U0084997

New Hotel English

新旅館英語
New Hotel English

by Mei-ling Cho
Bruce S. Stewart
John C. Didier
John H. Voelker
Kenyon T. Cotton

編者的話

　　本書雖定名為「新旅館英語」，但我想事先聲明一點，這不僅是飯店服務人員訓練英語會話必備專書，也是出國旅客住宿飯店時，利用它與飯店溝通的指南。

　　目前新式旅館已經開始採用電腦自動化作業，所以，入住登記手續也變得格外重要，旅客必須精通英語，以便將相關資料詳詳細細地告訴櫃柏接待人員，由他將所有資料打在電腦卡上。

　　薄薄的電腦卡取代了房門的鑰匙，進房時把卡片插進洞孔裡，門就會自動開啟；將卡片插進電源開關裡，燈才會亮，電視、冷暖氣、冰箱才有電。但一過結帳遷出日期，電腦卡就完全作廢，失去所有的功效。使用電腦卡時，務必仔細看清楚上面的英文說明，以免因絲毫差錯，而影響您的權益！

★語言不通是造成誤解的最大原因★

　　隨著商務的繁忙，觀光、自助旅行的盛行，出國的機會與日俱增，和旅館的接觸也越來越頻繁。從預約房間、辦理入住手續、貴重物品寄存保險櫃……乃至結帳退宿，若不懂得溝通

的技巧或處理不慎，往往會產生誤解和磨擦，造成旅途上的損失及不愉快。

本書第一篇「**旅客住宿飯店必備常識**」，告訴您如何以同等價錢取得條件較好的房間、遲到被取消預約的交涉方法、保險箱的使用規則、浴室裏的玄機、如何請總機安排叫醒電話等。這些小常識，是您住得舒暢的重要關鍵。

第二篇「**接待服務英語會話須知**」則詳細說明接待旅客時的會話注意事項、基本會話句型、及電話應對技巧，供旅館服務人員做為參考。

第三篇到第九篇為實況會話及活用例句，從預約、入住登記、分送行李、遲遲不見行李送來、寄存物品、遺失取物牌、確認難懂的姓名、請櫃柏傳話、廣播呼叫客人、說明洗衣服務時間、送洗衣物受損的處理……乃至處理旅客的抱怨等，應有盡有。

本書倘有疏失之處，祈各界先進不吝斧正。

旅 館 英 語

CONTENTS

第1篇　旅客住宿飯店必備常識

CHAPTER ❶——旅館住宿難題解決對策　　2

　　　　❷——自助旅行的規劃　　14

第2篇　接待服務英語會話須知

CHAPTER ❶——接待旅客英語會話注意事項　　22

　　　　❷——接待旅客基本英語會話句型　　26

　　　　❸——基本的電話應對　　38

第3篇　提送行李的服務 / BELLMAN SERVICES

CHAPTER ❶——帶領至櫃枱 / To the Front Desk　　44

　　　　❷——帶領至客房 / Check-in to Room　　46

　　　　❸——搭乘電梯 / Taking the Elevator　　48

　　　　❹——到達客房時 / Arriving at the Room　　51

　　　　❺——分送行李 / Standard Delivery　　54

　　　　❻——送錯行李時 / Delivery to the Wrong Room　　55

　　　　❼——回應客人的召喚 / Answering Calls　　58

　　　　❽——退宿時拿行李下樓 / Bringing Baggage down　　60

⑨──客人要求提取行李時 /

　　Picking up the Guest's Bags　　**63**

⑩──領取行李時 / Collecting One's Bags　　**65**

⑪──寄存物品時 / Depositing Some Items　　**67**

⑫──領取寄存物品時 / Collecting One's Items　　**69**

⑬──遺失取物牌時 / Tag Being Lost　　**70**

⑭──門房的應對 / Doorman's Service　　**73**

第4篇　訂房專線 / ROOM RESERVATIONS

CHAPTER ❶──來自國內的預約 /

　　Reservation from a Domestic Source　　**76**

❷──由第三者預約時 /

　　Reservation Made by a Third Party　　**79**

❸──來自國外的預約 /

　　Reservation from Overseas　　**83**

❹──想要的客房沒有空缺時 /

　　Desired Room Being Unavailable　　**85**

❺──旅館客滿時 / When the Hotel Is Full　　**87**

❻──無法連續預約至期滿 / Can't be Booked for All

　　the Nights Requested　　**90**

❼──提供差一等的客房 /

　　A Lower Quality Is Offered　　**93**

❽──詢問對房間視野的喜好 / Room View　　**94**

❾──詢問對房間類型的喜好 / Room Type　　**95**

⑩——床位大小及數目 /

　　Bed-size & Number in Room　　97

⑪——確認預約的電話 / Confirmation Call　　99

⑫——變更預訂的日期 /

　　Change of Reservation Date　　102

⑬——由第三者取消預約時 /

　　Cancellation by a Third Party　　104

第5篇　櫃檯(入宿登記)/ THE FRONT DESK (CHECK-IN)

CHAPTER ❶——入宿登記手續 / Check-in Procedure　　108

❷——尖峯時間的入宿登記 /

　　Check-in at a Busy Time　　111

❸——確認難懂的姓名 /

　　Confirmation of Difficult Surnames　　114

❹——由公司付帳的入宿登記 /

　　On a Company Account　　116

❺——顧客持有預付收據時 / With a Hotel Voucher　　119

❻——確認付款方式 /

　　Confirmation of Way of Payment　　121

❼——無預約記錄且旅館客滿時 /

　　When Reservation Can't Be Located　　123

❽——再度光臨而房間費不同時 / Room Rate Changes

　　for a Returning Guest　　126

❾——旅行團的入宿登記 / Tour Group Check-in　　129

　　對團體顧客的説明練習

第6篇　提供各項資料 / INFORMATION

CHAPTER ❶──詢問客房號碼時 /
Room Number Information　138

❷──所查詢姓名未列在表上 / The Name Doesn't
Appear on the List　140

❸──留言給住宿旅客 /
Message for a Staying Guest　142

❹──替客人傳話 / Guest Location　146

❺──介紹鄰近場所 / For Nearby Locations　149

❻──介紹較遠的場所 / For Faraway Locations　151

❼──指示客人如何到旅館 /
Giving Directions to the Hotel　152

❽──指示客人如何到目的地 /
Giving Directions to the Destination　154

❾──提供逛街觀光資料 / Information for Shopping &
Sightseeing　157

❿──親手遞交包裹 /
Delivery of Packages by Hand　159

⓫──代客人轉交信件 / Forwarding Letters　162

⓬──遞交・寄送郵件 /
Delivering & Sending Mails　165

⓭──廣播呼叫客人 / Paging　168

⓮──領取鑰匙時 / Picking up Room Key　170

⑮——因整修而要求客人換房間 /

Room Change Due to Repairs   172

⑯——想多住幾天卻沒有空房時 / Wishing to Extend One's

Stay But No Room Available   175

⑰——要求幫忙查詢電話號碼 /

Looking up a Telephone Number   178

第7篇　會計部門 / THE FRONT CASHIER

CHAPTER ❶——結帳退宿手續 / Check-out Procedure   182

❷——由公司付帳的情形 /

Check-out by Company Account   186

❸——解釋信用卡限額 /

Explaining Credit Limits   188

❹——標準滙兌手續 /

Standard Exchange Procedure   191

❺——說明夜間滙兌限額 /

Explaining the Night Change Limits   193

❻——保險櫃 / Safety Deposit Box   196

第8篇　客房管理部 / HOUSEKEEPING

CHAPTER ❶——說明洗衣服務時間 /

Explaining Laundry Service Hours   200

❷——洗衣服務受理程序 /

Laundry Reception Procedure   203

❸── 逾時送洗衣物 /

　　Too Late for That Day's Laundry　　206

❹── 需要乾洗時 / Dry-cleaned　　208

❺── 補綴和去污 / Mending & Stain Removal　　210

❻── 衣物分送錯誤 / Mis-delivery　　213

❼── 送洗衣物受損時 /

　　When Laundry is Damaged　　215

❽── 結帳後有物品遺留在房裏 / Checking out But Leav-

　　ing Some Items in the Room　　218

　　回覆詢問遺失物品的信函

❾── 請求清理房間 / Asking to Clean the Room　　224

❿── 借用電器設備 / Borrowing Equipments from

　　Housekeeping　　226

⓫── 客房服務 / Room Service　　228

⓬── 需要常備藥品時 /

　　Asking for Simple Medicine　　230

⓭── 提供報紙・香煙等服務 /

　　Services to the Room Guest　　232

⓮── 電視故障時 /

　　When TV is out of order　　235

⓯── 被鎖在防火道之外時 /

　　Being Locked out of the Fire Exit　　237

　　火災時疏散客人實用語句

　　地震時疏散客人實用語句

第9篇 轉接電話 / TELEPHONE OPERATORS

CHAPTER ❶──外線電話的處理 / Outside Calls　　　246

❷──客房沒有人回應時 /
No Reply from the Room　　249

❸──廣播呼叫客人 / Paging a Guest　　251

❹──被呼叫客人沒有回應時 /
No Reply from the Paged Guest　　253

❺──抵達時外線電話已掛斷 /
Outside Caller Being Cut off　　254

❻──客房間的通話與外線電話 /
Room-to-room & Outside Calls　　256

❼──早晨叫醒電話 / The Morning Call　　258

❽──代理通話服務 / Answering Service　　260

❾──對電話佔線的抱怨 /
Complaint about a Busy Line　　262

❿──越洋收聽人付費電話 /
Incoming Collect Call from Overseas　　264

⓫──越洋叫人電話 / Outgoing Overseas Person-to-
person Call　　267

⓬──直撥叫號電話 /
Station Call-Direct Dialing　　270

⓭──國際電話費用 / International Rates　　273

⓮──抱怨線路有雜音 /
Complaints about Noise on the Line　　275

Part 1

旅客住宿飯店
必備常識

旅館住宿
難題解決對策

　　講究「大」是全世界旅館流行的趨勢。大飯店已經由單純的旅客住宿所在，擴充而爲社交中心，強調旅客居住環境的品質。賓至如「歸」，這種像囘到家一樣的感覺，正是旅館期望帶給客人的服務目標。

　　然而，當您住宿旅館時，還是難免會碰到一些不如意的事。這可能是因爲經驗、常識不足所引起，也可能是外語溝通帶來的問題。對於出國業務考察、開會、觀光、探親的您，食宿的確是個大問題，而食宿卻又與飯店息息相關，密不可分。能住得舒暢，吃得愉快，有助於輕鬆順利達成商務目標，使您的旅遊完美無瑕，沒有任何缺憾。

　　本章擬就住宿飯店必備常識提出說明，提醒您注意一些容易出錯或造成損失的地方。

一、預約信函・E-mail範例

　　行程固定之後，就可以開始預約旅館，及早進行可避免向隅。如果時間充裕，可利用信函訂房，時間急迫的話，用E-mail比較省時。

　　歐式飯店以雙人床爲多，浴室多半只有淋浴設備，美式飯店則有浴盆及蓮蓬頭。所以，不論用信函或E-mail訂房，都要清楚指明欲住宿的房間類型、浴室設備、住宿時間、及班機抵達時間等。

◎ 國外訂房信（Room Reservation Letter）

E.M.I. ROYAL LONDON HOTELS
Leicester Square
London, WC2H 7NE England

Taipei, 01 June 2008

re: <u>Mrs. A. GLOOR/Dr. E. SEIDEL（2 pax）</u>

Dear Sir,

Reference is made to our above-mentioned clients and we
kindly ask you to reserve the following:

    1 suite with bath/WC
    from Oct. 28-Nov. 04, 2008

Arrival will be by China Airlines, flight CE 601 at 16.00h
ex Taiwan. We will send you our voucher-copy as soon as
we receive your confirmation indicating exact rate.

Looking forward to hearing from you soon we would like
to thank you in advance for your kind attention and remain.

                Yours faithfully
                TAIWAN BANK TRAVEL
                W. Liang

◉ E-mail 訂房

TO: Holidayhotel.com

FROM: jdoe@aol.com

DATE: June 23, 2008

SUBJECT: Reservation

Dear Sir/Madam:

This is Mandy Chang from Taiwan. I would like to reserve a double room with attached bathroom and A/C for two nights — May 30 and May 31. And I would prefer a room on the ground floor. I will arrive between 15:00 and 16:00. Please let me know if you have anything available as soon as possible. Thank you.

Sincerely,
Mandy Chang

Taiwan Taipei
jdoe@aol.com
Tel: 0912-983-157

二、善用訂房專線

　　旅行中如果未先預約飯店，確實令人頭痛，屆時還得拖著疲憊的身體和笨重的行李，到處奔波找尋住宿的地方。在觀光客多的城市，機場、火車站都設有預約飯店服務處，對他說 *"We need two rooms at an inexpensive hotel for tonight."*（我們要找一家不太貴的旅館，訂今晚兩間房。）就可以得到便宜、清潔的飯店名稱地址了。只要付一點手續費，由對方代辦預約即可。

　　此外，也可以利用電話洽詢是否有適合自己條件的房間，有些機場或車站還設有免費直撥電話。如果沒有預約服務處，也沒有飯店專用電話時，可從旅行指南（*Tour Guide*）、或當地的旅館雜誌（*Hotel Magazine*）中選好幾家飯店，再不然從電話簿中尋找亦可，然後打公用電話查詢是否有空房——*"Do you have one single room for two nights？"*（請問有可住兩晚的單人房嗎？）

三、越早登記房間越好

　　為避免產生有關房間的麻煩，最好早點登記，辦理入宿手續。付出的費用相同時，會按登記的順序，先分配出條件較好的房間。

　　有關個人對房間條件的要求，如床的大小及數目、房間的視野（看得到風景的）、房間的位置（不要靠近街道的）、浴室有無浴缸或淋浴設備等，在登記時就要說清楚。如此一來，在事前就可以消除一大半對房間的不滿了。

　　如果房間外面車聲太吵或電梯開關的聲響太大，設備不佳、房間鑰匙壞了，或房門開關不順，可以要求旅館換房間。

　　服務生負責搬運行李，帶領客人到房間，同時也有**確認客人對房間是否滿意的任務**。所以，不能輕易讓他離開，在他眼前檢視門鎖、燈光、冷暖氣或水龍頭等。如有任何不滿，馬上請他轉達給櫃枱。行李則暫時不要解開，換房間比較方便。

四、已經預約却因客滿被拒絕

　　一般來說，飯店的登記時間於午後六點截止。旅館的訂房確認函中，通常也都會列出：" *Room will be held until 6P.M. on the arrival date unless a later arrival is indicated.* "（房間只保留至抵達日下午六點，除非事先說明會晚到。）如果超過時間沒有預先聯絡，又碰到旅館客滿時，原先的預約就會被取消。

　　若因飛機等交通工具誤點，無法按預定時間抵達飯店，而被取消預約時，必須強調責任不在我方，據理力爭。" *We were on the plane. How could we call you from the sky* ? "（我們當時在飛機上，怎麼從空中打電話來？）

　　如果對方實在沒辦法調配出空房，可請其代爲詢問其他飯店，這比自己去找有效。此外，如果有旅行社的預約證明和預付收據，則可以避免發生這類事情。

五、在旅館裏遭竊怎麼辦？

　　飯店出入的人多，在大廳中被順手牽羊的情況不少。最普遍的是在櫃枱辦理入宿手續時，放在櫃枱上或脚邊的背包，一轉眼就不見了。卽使是團體旅行有導遊代辦登記手續，也不能掉以輕心。坐在沙發上聊天或眺望屋外，旁邊手提包不翼而飛的例子也不少。有時照相機放在桌上忘了拿，囘頭去取時已經無影無踪了。

這時要趕快找飯店的安全警衞或櫃枱：

"*Somebody took my camera from the counter*！"
（有人拿走了我放在櫃枱上的相機。）

"*My bag was stolen and my passport was in it*！"
（我的皮包被偸了，護照也在裏面。）

當然，最好能防患於未然，**背包、皮包應放在膝上，或抱在腋下**，若必須放在地上，要用雙脚夾住，相機則隨身背著，或放入袋中。

六、保險箱的使用規則

行李無論是在櫃枱附近被順手牽羊，或在房間內失竊，都必須自己負責，旅館只能儘力幫忙，但不負賠償責任。旅行箱即使上了鎖也不安全，有些小偷往往連箱一起帶走。爲了預防萬一，**貴重物品應寄存在旅館保險箱內。**

保險箱大都設在大廳一角，數目有限，但只要有空間都可免費利用。使用前先塡妥申請單，再向經辦人員提出申請。每個保險箱容積不同，但都可以用來保管現款及貴重物品，尤其是價格昂貴的珠寶、裝飾品等。但是如果不愼遺失保險箱鑰匙，就得賠償一定的金額。

以下爲台灣的旅館保險箱申請單背面所附的說明：

1. 如遺失此鑰匙,必須更換新鎖,價款新台幣 3,000 元,您須賠償半數 1,500 元。

2. 如果您退房遷離本飯店,而未將此鑰匙交回時,本飯店有權自行開啟並移出保存物品,不負任何責任。

1. If this key is lost, we will not only replace a new key but a new lock, which costs us NT$3,000 and you will be charged half the cost. Please take good care of the key.

2. The hotel management reserves the right to open the box and remove contents, without liability, if key is not surrendered when guest departs from hotel.

住客簽名 Guest Signature _____

房　　號 Room Number _____

日　　期 Date _____

七、飯店中應注意的禮節

1. 不可穿著睡袍和拖鞋出現在房間外的公共場所(走廊、餐廳、大廳)。

2. 到休閒飯店的游泳池或海濱,要走專用道路或搭乘專用電梯,不要穿著泳裝在公共走廊或大廳中行走。

3. 淋浴時必須拉好隔帘,以免把四周濺得滿地是水。水龍頭要記得關,不可使水溢出弄濕地毯。

4. 不可高聲喧嘩，或打開房門大聲吵鬧。

5. 對走廊擦身而過，或同搭電梯的人，都要打聲招呼。

6. 團體旅行時，外出囘來後到櫃枱領取房間鑰匙，切勿大夥兒擁擠著叫嚷自己的房間號碼，使服務人員手忙脚亂。

7. 有些飯店的大廳禁止照相，如拉斯維加斯（因大廳為賭場之故），最好不要故意違反規定。

八、浴室裏的玄機

要洗澡時發現沒有熱水是很令人懷惱的事。但別急著抱怨，很可能只是因為不了解冷熱水的標識或使用方法探致。

在英語系國家中，**熱水是 H（hot），冷水是 C（cold）**；拉丁語系國家則以 **C 表示熱水**，以 **F 表示冷水**；法語系國家以 **H 表示熱水**，**以 K 表示冷水**。最普遍的則是以紅色代表熱水，藍色代表冷水。也有以一個水龍頭來調節冷熱水的。

浴室中大型的毛巾是浴巾，中型的是擦拭身體用的，小型的用來擦臉，設淨身器的地方又有專用毛巾。

歐美許多旅館浴室內有 *bidet*（淨身器）的裝置，尤其是拉丁國家更為普遍。淨身器的構造不一，有的在洗淨盆中央設有小噴水器，有的在四周平均噴出熱水，有的兩者兼而有之。不管是哪一種，牆壁上都設有調節溫度的水龍頭，可隨時調節溫度和水量，因此要**面朝水龍頭的方向坐**。

放洗澡水時，因臨時有事外出，或太疲倦睡著了，而導致熱水滿過浴缸，由浴室溢出，弄濕房間的地毯，就得賠償飯店的損失。所以累了想睡覺時，務必關上水龍頭再睡；外出時則要記得檢查浴室水龍頭是否關好了。

九、提早結帳避免忙中有錯

結帳最擁擠的時段是早上八點到十點左右，往往大排長龍。若能避開這段尖峯時間，辦理結帳手續就方便多了。如果要在早上出發，可於前一天先結帳。儘早辦理有許多好處：

1. 帳目表有時會出差錯，**結帳時要花點時間仔細查看、核對一番**。若第二天急著趕時間，可能錯付別人的帳款，或多付了一些非自己簽帳的餐費、國際電話費等。有疑問時應當場問清楚：

   " *Is my overseas telephone call included in this bill*？"
   （我的國際電話包括在這張帳單裏了嗎？）

   " *I didn't have dinner at the hotel last night*."
   （昨晚我並沒有在旅館裏用餐。）

2. 若有貴重東西寄放在保險箱裏，匆忙之下可能會忘記領取。等半途發現再趕回來，反而就誤時間。

   結帳後發現有東西放在房間裏忘了拿，要趕快回去找櫃枱開房領取，如果已經抵達機場，也可以用電話聯絡飯店，若找到後送到何處。

   " *I have left my camera in room 981. Would you send it to ～, please*？"
   （我把相機忘在981號房了，請郵寄到～，好嗎？）

十、打國際電話

在旅館打國際電話，有經總機與直撥兩種。直撥比較方便，但是如果要打對方付費電話，或叫人電話，就得經過總機轉接了。

打國際電話時要考慮時差問題。

" *I want to call up Taipei . The Number is 907-1318 .*
The Area code is 02 ."

（我要打到台北，電話號碼是 907-1318，區域號碼是 02。）

在外國，有些新式的公用電話，只要準備足夠的硬幣，也可以打國際電話，這比在飯店打還要便宜。

十一、鑰匙——旅館內的信用卡

住在自動上鎖式的客房，應養成隨身攜帶鑰匙的習慣，走出房門前一定要證實鑰匙是否在身上。不管是自動鎖或非自動鎖，旅館的房門都有鎖鍊（ *door chain* ）、釣環（ *night latch* ）及防盜孔（ *peep hole* ）等安全設備。

把鑰匙放在屋內就關上房門，即是 " *I'm locked out .* "，應馬上請櫃枱人員用備用鑰匙（ *spare key* ）開門。但若您無法提出身份證明時，也會遭到拒絕。所以出門在外，務必隨身帶著能證明身份的文件。

在飯店內鑰匙就像信用卡一樣，用餐、購物、上美容院都可用以記帳，如果不小心遺失的話，至少要賠償200美元，不可不慎。

如果結帳離開之後，才發現沒有交還鑰匙，應馬上郵寄回去。

十二、叫醒電話及其他

　　早晨叫醒電話的英文爲 *morning call* 或 *wake-up call* ，想在明早六點半起床，可以告訴總機：" *I'd like to have a wake-up call at six-thirty tomorrow morning.* "但即使是白天或深夜任何時刻想起床，都可以委託總機用電話叫醒。

　　客房女侍每天早上會打掃客房、更換床單，如果不願被打擾的話，可以把印有" *Do Not Disturb.* "（請勿打擾）的卡片掛在門口。但是千萬注意不要掛反了，因爲其反面是" *Make up Bed.* "（請來舖床）。

十三、住宿旅館注意事項

⊙ 最好不要叫他 *bellboy*
　　大廳的角落設有幾個服務人員的位置，擔任旅客到達或出發時的行李搬運工作，及櫃枱交代的雜務。這些服務人員稱爲bellman。以前不論年紀大小一律稱爲bellboy 或 pageboy，但爲表示無輕視瞧不起之意，現在都統稱爲bellman。行李服務台領班稱爲bell captain，負責接聽電話，指派工作。

⊙ 寄存行李要記得索取保管收據
　　離開旅館做一次小旅行時，如果只外宿一夜或數夜，又將囘到同一旅館時，可以只帶走日常用品，而把不必隨身携帶的行李，暫時交由旅館保管，但務必要索取保管收據。

⊙ 旅館名片的妙用
　　外出時最好隨身携帶印有旅館名稱、地址及電話號碼等資料的名片或簡介等。如果不知道如何囘旅館時，就可以派上用場。

十四、小費及職司

在外國飯店中，不能期待在每家旅館，都能得到令人滿意的服務。所有的服務都是有價的，因此要有效運用小費。不過，**如果把委託對象搞錯，給小費也沒有用。**

飯店服務人員皆各司其職，有所要求時，要找對人，否則會被拒絕：

1. 門衞替客人開啓車門或雇計程車，並指揮門前的交通秩序。

2. 行李服務員負責行李搬運或寄存，遞送客人的物件、報紙、郵件、留言條，協助客人包紮包裹、稱重量等。

3. 行李服務員領班（ *bell captain* ）保管行李房鑰匙、代客購買車票、代辦出入境申請等服務。

4. 找娛姆、租車及旅遊、醫療，或想利用游泳池、網球場、保齡球館等設施，須與詢問台接洽。

5. 洗燙、乾洗、清掃房間可找客房服務部。

通常飯店內都備有服務指南（ *Directory of Services* ），供房客參考，以明瞭什麼狀況應該找誰。

豪華客房 Guest Room

自助旅行的規劃

　　自助旅行是現代時髦的旅遊潮流，可以個人單獨前往，也適合兩三知己或小家庭利用假期所作的精簡旅遊。傳統式的旅行團限制太多，而且蜻蜓點水式地走馬看好，無法滿足人們悠閒渡假的情趣。

　　自助旅行可以任意選擇出發日期，更可彈性增加停留的天數，以深入體會異國的風俗文化，參觀香港水上人家的生活、蒙地卡羅的賭場、暢遊美國大峽谷、約瑟里尼等著名國家公園，聆聽竹製管風琴的樂音，狂歡於巴西的嘉年華會，既是所有厭煩熙攘囂塵的都市人治療身心的特效藥，又可以行萬里路讀萬卷書。

　　但是行前有哪些必須的準備工作呢？

一、護照和簽證手續

　　申辦出國手續，可以委託經交通部觀光局核准有案的甲種旅行社代辦。如果自己有時間，可以親自去辦，最好在預定**出國前二個月**開始提出申請。若是首次申辦護照，可至外交部領事事務司（台北市濟南路一段 2 之 2 號，電話(02)3432888）辦理。應備文件如下：

1. 身分證正本

2. 白底彩色照片二張

3. 父或母或監護人之身分證正本

　　自從政府實施證照合一，將「入出境許可」加印條碼附貼於護照，且效期與護照相同而可多次使用後，國人今後出國即無需申請「出境證」，只要持有護照便可。若持舊式護照，仍須加貼入出境許可條碼，該許可須向內政部警政署入出境管理局（位於台北市廣州街 15 號，電話(02)2388-9393）申請。應備文件如下：

1. 申請書一份

2. 二吋照片 1 張

3. 國民身份證正反面影本一份

4. 國民身分證正本（驗畢退還）

5. 護照正面

　　要特別注意的是：護照必須親自簽名，不得由別人代簽。辦好護照後，即可著手辦理簽證（*Visa*）。

　　簽證是你要前往的國家允許你入境的證明，即外國政府核發的入境許可證。一般旅遊觀光簽證可分為免簽證、落地簽、須事先辦理簽證等三種。有邦交國家係向該國駐華大使館簽證組申辦，通常不另發文件，只在護照上蓋個戳記，由領事簽名即可。無邦交國家則向其授權的官方或半官方代理機構申請，須另外核發簽證文件。應備文件視前往國家而有不同的規定，但不外乎下列幾種：

1. 護照正本

2. 身分證影本

3. 來回機票或購票證明

4. 本人最近二吋正面半身脫帽照片若干張

5. 其他（如戶籍謄本、行程表、所得稅扣繳憑單、土地及房屋所有權狀等）

　　填寫申請表格時，務求整潔且確實無誤，申請表須自己簽名，**且應與護照簽名一致**。到美國在台協會申請非移民簽證時，必須提出證明你去美國的目的，及此行只是短暫訪問的有關證件。

　　一切準備就緒後，即可辦理出國結滙了。結滙必須親自辦理，攜帶護照（含簽證）、出境證、及欲結滙的金額，到中央銀行所指定的外滙銀行申辦。

　　申辦結滙金可用現金或銀行本票，惟用本票者須至開票銀行辦理，以購買少數小額現鈔備用，餘者以旅行支票爲宜。購得旅行支票後，**應立即在上款簽名，下款空白待使用時再副署**，切不可同時簽妥。因爲旅行支票上下款一經簽名即視同現金，一旦遺失，就無法掛失。

　　機票宜儘早購買並訂位，於出發前七十二小時再確認訂位。

二、旅行前的準備

　　出發前必須先規劃行程，整束裝備。選擇旅遊目標，擬定行程計畫表時，可至觀光協會、各大旅行社搜集免費的介紹刊物、地圖、及觀光指南等，先熟悉當地的交通、食宿狀況，安排路線，通常一個地點約停留三天，做放射狀的探索。此外，可以考慮把部分行程交由美國運通公司（*American Express*）或歐洲的湯姆士‧寇克公司（*Thomas Cook*）等旅行業者來安排，手續費相當低廉。

　　裝備以**質量輕、體積小、耐摔**爲原則，携帶太多物品常會有意外的缺失或開支，有些物品可視情形到當地再買。

三、小費

　　在國外旅行，除了飛機和公共汽車外，搭乘其他的交通工具，一律要給小費。乘船旅行時，在上岸前要親手將小費交給船艙服務員（*cabin boy*）、侍者（*waiter*）、甲板服務員（*deck boy*）、吧枱服務員（*bar boy*）等。至於金額多寡，可先和其他乘客商量。搭乘火車時也要給搬運工人、餐車內的侍者小費。雖然有些車站的搬運工人會以一件行李多少錢的方式要價，但原則上只有特別大或特別重的行李，才須付小費。

　　此外，計程車司機、理髮廳的師父、擦皮鞋或修指甲的人、高級劇院的領枱員、私人雇的觀光導遊、餐廳侍者等，舉凡要求其為個人服務者，都要付小費。

　　一般飯店通常在帳單上加進**餐費的10％至15％作為小費**，因此無須再多付小費。但是對侍者的服務感到特別滿意時，可以給額外的小費，金額當然因人而異，在美國通常是二十五分到一元之間。

　　這麼看來，小費也是一筆不容忽視的旅費，故必須隨身帶著數美元的小額貨幣。

四、貴重物品

　　出國時最好不要帶珠寶、金飾等貴重物品，但是總還**有護照、旅行支票**等重要物品，這些東西應該用小型塑膠封套收起來，放入衣服內面的口袋，或隨身攜帶的皮包裏，即使洗澡

時也必須帶進浴室裏，因為這兩樣東西是丟不得的。一丟就會寸步難行。

護照隨時都必須用到，兌換錢幣或購物時都可能用到它。到歐洲旅行時，更常碰到搭乘火車越過國境，而在車上接受海關人員檢查護照及行李的情況。

護照以外的貴重物品，到達旅館以後，可交由飯店保管。此時，必定要記得索取證明書或領取單。

五、住宿與飯店

規劃自助旅行時，應就行程的便利來安排住宿地點。原則上，除非當地有帳蓬出租，否則儘可能不要在外露營，以策安全（*有些國家公園晚上可能有熊或其他動物出沒*）。

為求經濟起見，可選擇住在國際性的*Namaste Hostel* 或汽車旅館（*motel*）、YMCA（*青年會*）或YWCA（*女青年會*）所經營的宿舍。Namaste Hostel 必須是會員才准住，住一晚約美金6～8元。

但是，有些Namaste Hostel 位於偏僻的郊外，倒不如在到達目的地後，從電話簿中挑選距離較近的旅館或YM（W）CA宿舍。YM（W）CA宿舍的價錢可能更便宜些。

如果不考慮經濟原因，當然以住旅館最方便。預約旅館房間要依行程來決定，旺季時最好要求回信加以確認。如果行程有所改變，一定要先通知旅館方面，以免造成對方的不便。此時，你可能必須負擔部份的損失。

　　如果沒有預約飯店，抵達時要找櫃枱確定是否有自己想要的房間（單人房或雙人房，*single room* or *double room*），有沒有衛浴設備（*with* or *without bath*）。如果有房間，在決定費用之後即可登記入宿。通常，在都市的飯店裏，**住宿費和餐費是分別計算的**。在自己房間內用餐要加一成（ 10 ％）的服務費。

　　若房間裏沒有衛浴設備，必須申請使用公共浴室，當然費用是另計的。

旅館客房部是與旅客接觸最頻繁的部門。有形的硬體設施（*facil-ities*），固然可以使旅客感到舒適便利，但軟體的服務（*service*），似乎更形重要。親切有禮的服務，才能使旅客稱心滿意。

客房部保有最正確的房間情況、最確實的帳單資料，並提供旅客有關郵電、鑰匙、電話、詢問、行李等服務。上設經理一人，主管整個旅館的房務。其下設有大廳副理及夜間經理。

夜間經理負責督導旅館夜班人員作業，維護旅館夜間的安全，預防及處理夜間旅客之意外，如酒醉或生病等。

大廳副理負責接受**旅客的抱怨**與不滿事項，解決支票背書事宜，防止意外事件、**接待貴賓**等。通常旅客與旅館會發生的糾紛不外乎：

1. 旅客貴重物品遺失——在房間、餐廳、公共場所或旅館的保險箱內遺失。

2. 旅客行李遺失——寄存在旅館遺失、協助搬運行李中遺失、無寄存遺失、打破行李箱或物品。

3. 旅客私自帶走或破壞房間的設備或用品。

4. 旅館的設施或管理不善，致使旅客受傷或受害——地板太滑、被電梯或自動門撞傷、無明顯的告示牌、破餐具割傷、傢俱不穩、衣服洗壞或燙壞、機器的聲音、車禍、中毒。

5. 旅客簽帳金額超過旅館規定，屢次催討却不付款。

6. 蓄意逃帳。

7. 要求以私人支票付帳。

8. **不守公共秩序**：酒醉、吵鬧、打架、賭博、色情。

9. 有訂房而無法安排房間。

Part 2

接待服務英語
會話須知

Restaurant Captain

接待旅客
英語會話注意事項

一、不要太顧及文法·針對情況應對作答

您認為英語很難、很麻煩嗎？俗語說「熟能生巧」只要多聽多講多練習，自然能說得很流利。最怕一開始就想要像中文一樣講得百分之百地完整、正確，而產生不敢開口或構思半天才作答的毛病。切記，**學英語會話最忌害羞**，英語並不是我們的母語，講錯了也不用難為情，只要能使對方瞭解自己想說的事，並且針對客人的問題作答，就已經相當不錯了。

剛開始時，不要存著非說得很流利不可的想法，**只要把握每一次說話的機會，就是進步的秘訣。**

二、用心聽客人說話·不懂時要再問一次

初學英文時，應先練習聽力，訓練自己的耳朵，以便跟得上客人的說話速度。

辦理預約時，在確定了客人的意思或要求的條件之後，應該覆誦一次，以表慎重。有不懂的地方要馬上再問一次——"*Pardon me*？"既簡單又管用。佯裝聽懂了，可能誤人誤己，是絕對行不通的。如果仍然不瞭解，則說"*Just a moment, please.*"然後找上級來應付。

三、慢慢地、清楚地說

所謂流暢的英語，並非要像雄辯家一樣地「口若懸河」，滔滔地說個不停。能將自己的意思正確簡潔地傳達給客人，就已經是旅館英語的上乘境界了。要注意**發音務必清楚、大聲**，語尾要夠明朗。

打招呼時聲音如果能夠很清楚，往後的會話也必然很流暢。除了大廳或餐廳的客人之外，對於走廊上擦肩而過的旅客，更應該養成展開笑臉打招呼的習慣。

四、不要使用和朋友交談式的英語

旅館英語會話，是以商用英語為基礎，必須正式、合乎禮節、具有格調，不可使用和朋友交談式的非正式英語。顧客至上，且旅館大部分是招待社會地位較高或經濟較充裕的階層，講話當然不能有失禮的地方。

旅館使用的既是正式的英語，故不會因為交談對象的年齡性別而有所改變。另外，要注意儘量避免使用和客人一樣的說話方式，使對方誤以為你在模仿。

以下列舉幾個例子，試比較正式英語和非正式英語的差別：

【非式正英語】	【正式英語】
What's your name?	*May I have your name, please?*
Do you want some tea?	*Would you like some tea?*
Over here, please.	*Could you come this way, please?*

五、不要使用俚語（*Slang*）

俚語對整個社會通常有直接或間接的影響，也是語言的一個重要組成部分。但是**俚語必須用於適當的場合**，對旅客使用俚語，會被認爲輕薄。像O.K., Sure, Yeah 等最好不要使用，應改成 " Certainly, sir. " 之類較爲莊重的說法。

六、不要說 " *I don't know.* "

客人通常是有事相求或遇到麻煩時，才會開口詢問，如果以「不知道」一口加以回絕，會顯得很不親切。外籍旅客或部分長期居住海外的華僑，由於語言不通，所以常會有不安的感覺，有事情或麻煩時更需要有人伸出援手，一句 " I don't know." 只會使他更不知所措。**適時加以協助，才能建立旅館服務親切的形象**。如果客人詢問的東西自己不懂的時候，馬上說 " *Just a moment , please . I'll check that for you.* " （請稍等，我查一查。），然後去請敎別人，或許也可以由瞭解的人代爲解答。

七、眼睛也能說話

「說話的時候眼睛要看著對方」——這是世界各國共通的原則。尤其是西歐，說話的時候如果不看著對方，會被認爲說謊，或是對自己所說的話沒有自信。

卽使你滿懷誠意和對方交談，眼睛却盯著下面看，或左右顧盼，對方必然無法感受到你的誠意。**不管客人是多麼地生氣，你都應該看著他的眼睛，虛心地聽他說話**。如此一來，至少能平息對方 30％的怒火，自然我方的回答或解釋說明，也比較容易得到客人的理解。

但，如果過分盯著客人看，有時候會導致反效果。應該適度點頭附和，並配合誠摯、體貼的表情。

八、注意手勢的使用

在表達意思的時候，語言只能傳達全部的35％。有些事情在電話中沒辦法解決，但當面洽談却能馬上迎双而解。這是因爲臉部的表情和動作能表達語言所不能傳達的意思。**面對很難溝通的外國人時，加上手和身體的動作，有助於意思的表達和溝通。**

但是，要特別注意手勢的使用，因爲手勢所代表的意思會因民族、習慣而有差異。不過，指示方向時，則不會有任何差異，可放心使用。

九、對女客人，不論年齡都可以用ma'am

如衆所週知，男客人用 *sir* 稱呼，女客人則以 *ma'am*〔mæm；mɑm〕稱呼，ma'am 是 *madam* （女士；夫人——對女子的尊稱）的俗稱。年輕的女客人如果以中文稱呼她「女士」，多少會有些奇怪的感覺，但 ma'am 的使用則與年齡無關。

另外，在招呼客人時，最好用 *Excuse me, sir* （或 *ma'am* ）。切忌以 Mr. 或 Miss.相稱。在招呼小客人時，可以只用 Excuse me. 但不可以稱呼小客人爲 *Boy* 或 *Girl* 。

TAIPEI 國賓大飯店
THE AMBASSADOR HOTEL

接待旅客
基本英語會話句型

一、四種基本句型

正式的英語，疑問句只有下列四種句型：

May I ~？（我可以～嗎？）　　*Could you~*？（您可以～嗎？）

Would you ~？（您願意～嗎？）　*Shall I ~*？（我可以～嗎？）

這四種基本句型被廣泛地應用在業務應對上。用法如下：

1. 自己想做某些事情時，用 May I ~? 想問不知道該不該問的問題時，用 May I know？

> ・*May I* have your name, please？ 請問貴姓？
>
> ・*May I* have your check-out time, please？
> 　請問您什麼時候要結帳退宿？
>
> ・*May I* see your passport, please？
> 　請讓我看看您的護照好嗎？
>
> ・*May I know* your nationality, please？
> 　我可以請問您的國籍嗎？

2. 有求於客人時，用 Could you～？

> • *Could you* fill out the form, please？
>   請填寫這張表格好嗎？
>
> • *Could you* write that down, please？
>   請寫下來好嗎？
>
> • *Could you* draft the telegram, please？
>   請擬好電報的草稿好嗎？
>
> • *Could you* hold the line, please？
>   請不要掛斷電話好嗎？

以上這類情況如果用 Would you～？ 來問，就變成上級對下級說話的口氣，帶有質問對方的意思，不適合旅館服務人員使用，所以應該特別留意。

3. 詢問客人的喜好或意願時，用 Would you～？

> • *Would you* like tea or coffee？ 您要茶還是咖啡？
>
> • *Would you* like to take a taxi？
>   您要不要搭計程車？
>
> • *Would you* mind ～ing？
>   您介意～嗎？ ——用於徵求對方同意時

下列為「疑問詞＋Would you～？」的句型，只能用於詢問客人的希望。

- When *would you* like to visit the Palace Museum?
  您什麼時候要參觀故宮博物院？

- Where *would you* like to have lunch？
  您想去哪裡吃午餐？

- What time *would you* like to eat？
  您想要什麼時候用餐？

- Who *would you* like to contact？
  您想和誰聯絡？

- Why *would you* like to visit Hong Kong？
  您為什麼想去參觀香港？

- Which kind of room *would you* prefer？
  您喜歡哪一種房間？

- Which museum *would you* like to visit？
  您想去參觀哪一間博物館？

- How *would you* like to settle your bill？
  您想用什麼方式付帳？

- How much money *would you* like to spend？
  您打算花多少錢？

- How long *would you* like to stay？
  您要停留多久？

- How many tickets *would you* like to buy？
  您要買幾張票？

4. 提供意見或服務給客人時，用 Shall Ⅰ～? 與 Would you like me to do ～? 的意思相同。

- *Shall I* draw the curtains？要我把窗帘拉上嗎？
- *Shall I* call a bellman？要我叫服務生來嗎？
- *Shall I* draw you a map？要我畫張地圖給您嗎？
- *Shall I* make the reservation for you？
  要我替您訂房間嗎？

二、打招呼

看見客人應該由我方先打招呼。打招呼的方式是在

　　Good morning, ～.（早上）

　　Good afternoon, ～.（下午；正午十二時以後）

　　Good evening, ～.（下午六時以後）

這些句型之後，應狀況所需，加入適當的文句，例如：

- *Good afternoon*, sir. *Welcome to* the Grand
  Hotel. 先生，午安。歡迎光臨圓山大飯店。
- *Good evening*, ma'am. *May I help you*？
  夫人，晚安。需要我效勞嗎？
- *Good morning*, sir. *Are you checking out*？
  先生，早安。您要結帳嗎？

如果知道顧客姓氏，也可以直呼某某先生。在電話的對答中，可以在後面直接加上公司名或部門名稱，如：

> - *Good morning*, sir. This is Lai Lai Sheraton Hotel Taipei. 先生，早安。這裡是來來大飯店。
> - *Good morning*, sir. This is the Front Desk. May I help you？
>   先生，您早，需要我效勞嗎？

然而，若過分使用 sir 或 ma'am 可能會引起反效果，所以應該依狀況所需作適當的省略。

三、回答

在與客人對話過程中，有時必須就對方要求的事項作簡約而具體的說明，有時須隨聲附和表示認同，或確認客人所說的話，以表示慎重。仔細聽、聽清楚，再依狀況作正確的回答尤爲重要。

1. 一般的回答

> - I see, sir. 我了解，先生。
> - Certainly, sir. 當然好的。

2. 要客人等待時

> - Just a moment, please. 請稍等。
> - Thank you for waiting, sir. 先生，讓您久等了。
> - Could you wait a little longer, please？
>   請稍候一下好嗎？

3. 拒絕客人所求時

在沒辦法符合客人的要求，而想加以拒絕的時候，不可以直接說
No，～，而應該用下面的說法，並在其後加上理由說明。

- I'm afraid ～　抱歉，很不巧～
- Excuse me，sir～　先生，對不起～

---

4. 道歉的時候

說話時注視著客人的眼睛，是非常重要的禮節。此外，措辭中應
該避免連續使用含有「對不起」之類的語氣。
如果是自己的錯失，用 I am ～．如果是為飯店的錯誤而道歉，
則用 We are ～．

- *I'm very sorry for* the delay.
  很抱歉耽誤您的時間。
- *I'm very sorry for* the inconvenience.
  很抱歉給您帶來不便。
- *I'm very sorry for* the mistake.
  很抱歉弄錯了。
- *I'm very sorry to* hear that. 聽到這個消息我很
  難過。——並非因自己的過失而道歉
- *I would like to apologize for* ～．
  我要為～道歉。——上級負責人使用的措辭

---

5. *Yes*, *No* 的使用方法

Yes 和 No 的使用方法，務請特別留意。肯定的疑問句，回答 Yes 意思爲「是的」，回答 No 意思爲「不」。但是換成否定的疑問句，情況就恰好相反了，回答 Yes 意思爲「不」，回答 No 意思爲「是的」。請參考以下例句，就可以很容易瞭解。

例：假設盒子是紅色的（ The box is red. ），其對答如下：

① *Is* the box red ?　　　　　Yes, it is. 是的。

② The box is red, *isn't* it ?　Yes, it is. 不,是紅的。

③ *Isn't* the box red ?　　　Yes, it is. 不,是紅的。

④ The box isn't red, *is* it ?　Yes, it is. 是的。

⑤ The box is *black*, *isn't* it ?　No, it isn't. 是的,不是黑色的。

旅館英語中，常用的 Yes，No 回答句如下：

• *Do* you have a single room for tonight ?
　你們今晚有單人房嗎？

Yes, we do. 是的，有。　　*No*, we don't. 不,沒有了。

• *Don't* you have a single room for tonight ?
　你們今晚沒有單人房了嗎？

Yes, we do. 不，還有。

I'm afraid, we don't. 恐怕沒有了。

• *Would you mind* if I open the curtains ?
　您介意我拉開窗簾嗎？

Yes, I would. 不用麻煩了。

No, not at all. 好的，請便。

---

6. 客人說 Thank you. 時的回答

有下列幾種回答，可隨意應用。

- You are welcome. 不客氣。
- Not at all. 不客氣。
- Thank you, sir. 謝謝您，先生。
- Thank you very much. 非常謝謝。

---

7. 給客人東西的時候

有下列幾種說法，都表示「請拿去」的意思。

- Here is your room key. 這是您的房間鑰匙。
- Here you are. 您要的東西在這裡。
- Here it is. 這就是。

---

8. 送客人離開的時候

根據狀況有下列幾種說法：

- Have a nice day. 祝您一天都愉快。
- Have a good night. 晚安。──不可以用 good sleep
- *Please enjoy your stay*. 祝您住得愉快。
- We hope you have enjoyed your stay.
  希望您住得還滿意。──結帳時用
- *We hope to see you again soon*. 歡迎很快再度光臨。
- Thank you for staying with us. 謝謝光臨。

四、不懂得客人的英語時

客人有所要求或疑問時，應該儘量幫忙或加以解釋說明，有聽不懂的時候，不可一味地裝懂，應該馬上再問一次，或是說 Just a moment, please，然後找上級或英語能力較高的人代為回答。

另外，不習慣客人的英語，可能是因為不瞭解其中的意思。所以，應該把握話中的關鍵字，如此必然有助於理解語意。

1. 不易聽懂的時候

此時應請對方覆述一次，說法如下：

> * *Pardon me* ? 原諒我，請再說一次。
> * I beg your pardon ? 原諒我，請再說一次。
> * Could you repeat that, please ? 請再說一次好嗎？
> * I'm afraid I don't understand. 我恐怕不了解。
> * *Could you speak more slowly*, please ?
>   請說慢一點好嗎？

2. 不易瞭解的時候

不瞭解的地方可以再詢問一次，或者以自己的說法重覆客人所說的話，以證實您的瞭解無誤。

> * Excuse me, sir. *Do you mean*～?
>   對不起，先生。您的意思是～嗎？

五、數字的讀法

① 13～19 的字尾是 " ***teen*** " , 例如13為 thirteen , 14為 fourteen 。

② 從20至90表十位數字的字尾是 " ***ty*** " , 如 30為 thirty , 40為 forty 。

③ teen 和 ty 很容易搞混 , 應該特別注意發音是否正確 。

④ ***hundred*** (一百)的後面須加 ***and*** (但美語 and 可以省略) , 如果百位數為零 , 要在 thousand (一千)後面加上 and 。

          139元 : one hundred ***and*** thirty-nine dollars

     1,028元 : one thousand ***and*** twenty-eight dollars

     2,300元 : Two thousand three hundred dollars.

⑤ 自 1,000 至 1,999 的數字有兩種讀法 :

                one thousand four hundred and fifty-six
    1456 :
                fourteen hundred and fifty-six

    4,250元 : *Four thousand two hundred **and** fifty dollars.*

            (*Forty two hundred* and fifty dollars. 美語也有這種讀法)

⑥ " 萬 " 的讀法 , 在 thousand 前面加上十位數或百位數 。

    53,752元 : Fifty-three thousand seven hundred and fifty-two dollars.

⑦ 數目很大時 , 先從右邊算起 , **每三位數歸在一起** , 從最左邊的三位數開始唸起 , 每三位數唸完之後 , 須加上單位名稱 。

$$\underbrace{1\ 2\ 3}_{\uparrow} ,\quad \underbrace{4\ 5\ 6}_{\uparrow} ,\quad \underbrace{7\ 8\ 9}$$

million thousand

（讀法） One hundred and twenty-three million
    four hundred and fifty-six thousand
    seven hundred and eighty-nine.

⑧ 年號的讀法是每兩位數合併爲一段落。

 1987年　nineteen eighty-seven

⑨ 時間的讀法

 三點鐘：three o'clock
 五點半：five thirty 或 half past five
 九點十五分：nine fifteen 或 a quarter past nine
 九點四十五分：nine forty-five 或 a quarter to ten

⑩ 電話號碼的讀法

 8503244　eight, five, 0, three, two, double four
 2177387　two, one, double seven, three, eight, seven

⑪ 樓的讀法

 第21樓：the twenty-first Floor
 第17樓：the seventeenth Floor

⑫ 住址的讀法

 426 Maple Avenue：four twenty-six Maple Avenue
 1400 16th St.：fourteen hundred, Sixteenth Street

⑬ 百分比、折扣的讀法

    20％： twenty percent

    0.4％： point four percent

    八折： twenty percent discount

    九五折： five percent discount

⑭ 其 它

    1.3   one point three

    3分之1   one third（分子用基數，分母用序數）

    3分之2   two thirds（分子大於2時,分母須加"s"以形成
                            複數形）

    5分之3   three fifths

基本的電話應對

一、電話應對的禮貌

電話交談沒辦法以表情或動作傳達意思。因此,如果應對不適當,很容易招致對方的誤解。基本的應對原則如下,請謹記在心。

- 電話鈴響馬上拿起話筒。
- 第一聲就要使對方留下深刻印象。
- 將對方當成在自己眼前,說話時如平常般殷勤、懇切。
- 過分殷切,可能引起對方不愉快的反應。
- 說話要掌握適當的速度和深入的要領。
- 少說一般不常用的簡縮語或專門術語等。
- **重要事項應邊說邊作筆記**,並且復誦一次以求慎重(如時間、人數等)。
- 自己不懂時,應找人代勞。
- 不懂的事不可佯裝瞭解而回答對方。
- 無法立即答覆的時候,**應先取得對方的連絡處**,再掛上電話。
- 處理重大事項或特殊事件,應徵得上司同意。
- 不管多麼忙碌,也應親切、冷靜地應付。
- 長途電話或國際電話應長話短說。

・確定對方掛了電話之後，再輕輕掛上話筒。
・卽使是公司同事的電話，也應親切地應對。

二、拿起話筒時的會話

商業電話的應對，通常拿起話筒之後先打招呼，接下來說明我方的名號、單位以及名字。這時候可以不用說"喂！"直接說"早安，這裏是××飯店。"。

如果對方來的電話說英語，因爲我方第一聲仍用中文，所以會有如下的對話方式出現。

「詢問台，您好。」

" Is this the Information Desk？"（這裏是詢問台嗎？）

" Speaking. May I help you？"（是的，需要我效勞嗎？）

另外，商業電話通常不說 Hello！（以 " *Is that（this）*～？ " 詢問時，美語經常以 " *Yes, it is.* "回答。）

三、撥錯電話的時候

對方撥錯電話的時候，應採下列的應對方式：

> ・ I'm afraid *you have the wrong number*. This is the China Hotel, 331-9521.
> 　您恐怕撥錯號碼了。這裏是 331-9521，中國大飯店。

如果是接線作業的錯誤，應該立卽轉換到對方想連絡的單位。

- This is Room Reservations. *I'll transfer your call to* Restaurant Reservations.

  這裏是客房預約部，我幫您轉到餐廳訂席部。

- *I'm afraid this is a direct line.* We cannot transfer your call to the Western Restaurant. Could you dial 234-5677, please?

  抱歉，這是直撥電話。我們沒辦法爲您轉到西餐廳，請您撥 234-5677，好嗎？

- I'm afraid we cannot transfer calls from the house phones. *Could you dial extension 33 directly*, please?

  館內電話恐怕無法換線，請您直接撥33號分機,好嗎？

四、當事人不在的時候

- I'm afraid Mr. Wang is out at the moment. *He should be back around 5 p.m.*

  王先生現在恐怕不在。他會在下午五點左右囘來。

- I'm afraid Mr. Lee is not at his desk now. *He should be back in 10 minutes.*

  李先生現在恐怕不在他的座位上。十分鐘後他應該會囘來。

- I'm afraid *Mr. Lin is on another line.* Could you hold the line, please?

  林先生正在講電話，請稍等一下，好嗎？

- I'm afraid *Mr. Liu is in a meeting at the moment*. It should be over at 3:30 p.m., sir.
  劉先生現在恐怕正在開會。會議預定在下午三點半結束。
- I'm afraid Mr. Cho is in another room. *I'll transfer your call. Could you hold the line,* please？卓先生在別間房間裏，我幫您轉過去，請稍等一下，好嗎？
- *I'll tell him to call you back when he returns.* 等他回來我會叫他回電給您。
- May I have your name and phone number, please？請問您貴姓和電話號碼？

沒辦法立卽答覆時，可參照下列的説法：

- I'm afraid we cannot give you an answer at the moment. *May we call you back*？
  現在恐怕無法給您答覆，我們可以再連絡嗎？
- *Where can we contact you*？
  我們可以在哪裏聯絡到您？（英語單字沒有連絡處這個字。所以用這種表達方式）

五、會話結束時

電話應對結束時，可以說和開頭同等重要。尤其有關接待客人的服務，因爲此後還要繼續交易。所以會話終結使用的字眼應該簡潔有力，給對方良好的印象。（最好不要説 *Bye-bye*。）

- ***Thank you for calling***. 謝謝您來電。

- You're welcome, sir.

  不客氣，先生。（ Thank you. 的回答 ）

- ***We look forward to hearing from you***.

  我們期待聽到您的消息。

- We look forward to another chance to serve you.

  我們期待另有機會為您服務。（ 不合客人要求的時候 ）

- We're very sorry we couldn't help you, sir.

  很抱歉沒辦法為您服務。

- Thank you, sir. Goodbye.

  謝謝您，先生。再見。（ 用於一般會話結束時 ）

- Not at all. 不客氣。（ 對撥錯電話者的應答 ）

另外，在受理預約的作業上，臨結束前受理預約的職員會自報姓名，通常在報過姓名之後，會在 My name is 之後，加上如下的客套話：

- ***We look forward to serving you***.

  我們期待為您服務。

- ***Please contact me*** if you have any further questions.

  如果有任何問題請跟我連絡。

Part 3

提送行李的服務
Bellmen Services

帶領至櫃枱

To the Front Desk

~~《 **對話精華** 》~~

◉ Welcome to the Ambassador Hotel. 歡迎到國賓大飯店。

◉ How many pieces of luggage do you have？
您有多少件行李？

◉ I'll show you to the Front Desk. This way, please.
我帶您到櫃枱，請跟我來。

Dialogue： *B* ＝ **Bellman**（為旅客搬送行李的）服務生　*G* ＝ **Guest** 旅客

B：Good evening, sir. *Welcome to the Ambassador Hotel*.

B：先生，晚安。歡迎到國賓大飯店。

G：Thank you.

G：謝謝。

B：*How many pieces of luggage do you have*？

B：您有多少件行李？

G：Just these three.

G：只有這三件。

B：Two suitcases and one bag. Is that right？

B：兩個旅行箱和一個袋子，對嗎？

G：Yes. That's all.

G：是的，就這些。

B：*I'll show you to the Front Desk. This way*, please.

B：我帶您到櫃枱，請跟我來。

I will put your bags by the post over there.

我把您的袋子放在那兒的柱子旁邊。

G: I see, thanks.

G：好的，謝謝。

B: A bellman will show you to your room when you have finished checking in.

B：您辦完住宿登記時，服務生會帶您到房間去。

G: O.K. Fine.

G：好的。

B: *Please enjoy your stay.*

B：請好好休息。

活 用 練 習

① How many bags do you have? 您有多少件行李？

② *Could you check in at the Reception Counter over there*, please?
請到那邊的接待處辦理住宿登記，好嗎？

③ This is the Reception Counter where you check-in.
這是您辦理住宿登記的接待處。

④ I'm afraid it is very crowded now. *Could you wait in line, please*？現在恐怕很擠，請排隊等候好嗎？

⑤ Could you stand in line for registration, please?
請排隊登記好嗎？

** *front desk* 櫃枱　　luggage〔'lʌgɪdʒ〕*n.* 行李
　　post〔post〕*n.* 柱子　　*check in*（到達旅館時）住宿登記
　　reception counter 接待處（即接待客人，客人詢問房間等事務的櫃枱）
　　crowd〔kraʊd〕*v.* 擁擠　　**registration**〔,rɛdʒɪ'streʃən〕*n.* 登記

2

帶領至客房
Check-in to Room

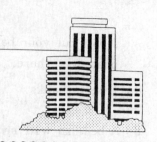

〔 對話精華 〕

◈ I'll *show* you to your room. 我帶您到房間去。

◈ Is there anything *valuable* or *breakable* in your bag?
您的袋子裡有什麼貴重或易碎的東西嗎?

Dialogue: *B* = Bellman (為旅客搬送行李的)服務生　*G* = Guest 旅客

B : Good evening, sir. *I'll show you to your room*. You have two suitcases and one bag. Is that right?

B : 先生,晚安。我帶您到房間去。您有兩個旅行箱和一個袋子,對吧?

G : Yes, that's right.

G : 對的。

B : *Is there anything valuable or breakable in your bag*?

B : 您的袋子裏有什麼貴重或易碎的東西嗎?

G : Yes, there's a bottle of whisky.

G : 有,有一瓶威士忌。

B : Could you carry this bag, sir? I'm afraid the contents might break.

B : 先生,您自己提這個袋子好嗎?我怕裏面的東西會破。

G : Sure, no problem.

G : 好的,沒問題。

B：Thank you, sir. *May I have your room key*, please？

G：Yes. Here you are.

B：Thank you, sir. Your room is on the 12th Floor.
Please follow me.

B：謝謝您，先生。請給我房間的鑰匙好嗎？

B：好的，在這兒。

G：謝謝您，先生。您的房間在12樓，請跟我來。

活 用 練 習

1　*May I help you with your bags*, sir？先生，我幫您提行李好嗎？

2　*Just a moment*, please. I'll bring a baggage cart.（英國用 trolley）請稍等，我去拿一輛行李車。

3　Is this your baggage？這是您的行李嗎？

4　Is this all your baggage？這是您所有的行李嗎？

5　*Is this all you have*？這是您所有的東西嗎？

6　*Would you mind taking these bottles with you*？
您介意自己拿這些瓶子嗎？

7　Could you take this camera with you, sir？
先生，您自己拿這台照相機好嗎？

** valuable〔'væljuəbl̩〕*adj.* 貴重的　　breakable〔'brekəbl̩〕*adj.* 易碎的
content〔'kɑntɛnt〕*n.*（常為複數）內容；所容之物
baggage〔'bægɪdʒ〕*n.* 行李（ *baggage* 通用於**美國**， *luggage* 通用於**英國**，但
近年來美國亦用 *luggage* ，尤指昂貴之小件行李。兩者皆為不可數名詞。
baggage cart 行李車＝ trolley〔'trɑlɪ〕)　　　item〔'aɪtəm〕*n.* 物品

搭乘電梯
Taking the Elevator

~~~ *對話精華* ~~~

◉ Please take the elevator *on your right*.
請搭乘您右邊的電梯。

◉ *After you*, sir. 先生，您先上。

Dialogue: *B* = **Bellman** （為旅客搬送行李的）服務生　*G* = **Guest** 旅客

B： *Your elevator is this way*.

G： I see.

B： The elevators on the right
are the express ones to
the tenth Floor and above.
The elevators on the left
go to the tenth Floor only.
They stop at every floor.
Your room is on the
twelfth Floor. *Please take
the elevator on your right*.
After you, sir.

G： Thanks.

B：您的電梯在這邊。

G：哦。

B：右邊是10樓以上的直達電
梯。左邊的電梯只到10樓，
每一樓都停。您的房間在12
樓，請搭乘您右邊的電梯。
先生，您先上。

G：謝謝。

B : Is this your *first visit to* Taiwan, sir ?

G : Yes, it is.

B : I hope that you will *enjoy your trip*. This is the twelfth floor. Your room is to the right. *After you*, sir.

(*Gets out of elevator*)

B : *This way*, please.

B : 先生，這是您第一次來台灣嗎？

G : 是的。

B : 希望您旅途愉快。這是12樓，您的房間在右邊。先生，您先走。

（ 走出電梯 ）

B : 請走這邊。

活 用 練 習

☆ 電梯內的話題

1 How was your trip ? 旅行愉快嗎？

2 *How do you like Taipei* ? 您覺得台北怎麼樣？

3 You must be tired. 您一定很累了。

☆ 上下電梯時

1 Just a moment, please. *The elevator will be here soon.* 電梯馬上就來，請稍等。

2 Watch your step, please. 請小心走。

3 Going up, sir. (Going down, sir.) 上去，先生。（下去，先生。）

④ Next car, please. (人滿了)請搭下一班。

⑤ Please **take this elevator for** the restaurant.
請搭這部電梯去餐廳。

⑥ Are you going up (down), sir? 先生,您要上(下)去嗎?

⑦ **Which floor,** sir? 到哪一樓,先生?

⑧ This doesn't stop at the second floor. 二樓不停。

⑨ This elevator does not go up to the guest rooms.
這部電梯不到客房。

⑩ **It is an express elevator for** the restaurants.
這是直達餐廳的電梯。

⑪ If you would like to go to the restaurants on the top floor,
please change elevators at the 15th Floor.
如果您想上頂樓的餐館,請在15樓換電梯。

⑫ After you, sir. (Go ahead, please.) 先生,您先請。

** **elevator** 〔'ɛlə,vetɚ〕 *n.* 電梯
express 〔ɪk'sprɛs〕 *adj.* 直接的;快速的
restaurant 〔'rɛstərənt〕 *n.* 餐館

到達客房時
Arriving at the Room

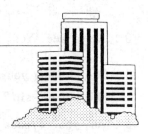

〔 對話精華 〕

◎ May I put your bags here？我可以把行李放在這兒嗎？

◎ Just put them anywhere. 隨便攤著吧。

◎ Will you get me the cable form？
　幫我拿電報表格來好嗎？

◎ All stationeries are in this desk drawer.
　所有的文具都在這個書桌抽屜裡。

Dialogue： *B* = **Bellman** （為旅客搬送行李的）服務生　*G* = **Guest** 旅客

B： This is your room.

　　（ *Unlocks door and switches*
　　on light ）

　　After you, sir. ***May I put***
　　your bags here？

G： Sure. Just put them any-
　　where.

B： Here is your room key. ***Is***
　　this the correct number
　　of bags？

B：這是您的房間。

　　（ 打開門鎖，捻亮電燈 ）

　　先生，您先走。我可以把行
　　李放在這兒嗎？

G：當然可以。隨便攤著吧。

B：這是房間的鑰匙。行李的件
　　數正確嗎？

G : Let's see. Yes, that's all.

G : 我看看。對,就是這些。

B : May I hang your coat in the closet, sir ?

B : 我把您的外套掛進壁櫥裏好嗎?

G : Ah, yes. *Please do*!

G : 嗯,好的。麻煩你!

B : Shall I *open the curtains* for you ?

B : 要我幫您打開窗簾嗎?

G : Yes, that's a good idea.

G : 好的,眞是好主意。

G : I want to send a cable, will you get me the cable form ?

G : 我要拍一通電報,幫我拿電報表格來好嗎?

B : *All stationeries are in this desk drawer*, sir.

B : 先生,所有的文具都在這個書桌抽屜裡。

G : That's fine. I'll call you when it is ready.

G : 好,我寫好時會叫你過來。

B : Yes, sir. *Anything else* (*I can do*), sir ?

B : 是的,先生。還有別的事嗎?

G : No, I guess that's all (*for the time being*).

G : 沒有了,(暫時)就這樣。

活 用 練 習

1. Shall I *turn* the cooling *up* ?

   要我把冷氣調強一點嗎？

2. Shall I *turn* the cooling (heating) *down* ?

   要我把冷（暖）氣調弱一點嗎？

3. Room Service is *available* from 6 a.m.

   從早上六點起就可以利用客房服務。

4. The Coffee Shop serves breakfast from 6 a.m. until 10 a.m.

   咖啡廳從早上六點起供應早餐，一直到十點打烊。

5. Here is a *brochure* explaining hotel services.

   這兒有說明飯店服務的手冊。

** **unlock**〔ʌnˈlɑk〕*v*. 開（門）鎖
   switch〔swɪtʃ〕*v*. 扭開（閉）電燈
   closet〔ˈklɑzɪt〕*n*. 櫥子
   curtain〔ˈkɜˈtn̩〕*n*. 窗帘
   cable〔ˈkebl̩〕*n*. 電報
   stationery〔ˈsteʃənˌɛrɪ〕*n*. 文具
   drawer〔drɔr〕*n*. 抽屜
   for the time being " 暫時 "
   available〔əˈveləbl̩〕*adj*. 可利用的
   brochure〔broˈʃʊr〕*n*. 小冊子
   explain〔ɪkˈsplen〕*v*. 解釋

分送行李
Standard Delivery

╟ **對話精華** ╟

🔺 I have brought your baggage. 我幫您把行李送來了。

🔺 The department store has delivered a box for you.
百貨公司送過來一箱東西要給您。

🔺 Could you sign here, please? 請在這兒簽名好嗎？

Dialogue: G = **Guest** 旅客　　B = **Bellman** (爲旅客搬送行李的) 服務生

G : Yes, coming. Who is it ?

G : 來了，哪一位？

B : The Bellman, sir. *I have brought your baggage.*

B : 先生，我是服務生，幫您把行李送來了。

G : Fine. Come on in !

G : 好的，請進。

B : *We're very sorry for the delay,* sir. May I put it (*your bags*) here ?

B : 對不起，先生，耽擱了一下。我把行李放在這兒好嗎？

G : Sure.

G : 好的。

B : Is this everything, sir ?

B : 先生，這是所有的行李嗎？

G : Yes, that's right.

G : 是的。

B : *Enjoy your stay with us,* sir.

B : 先生，好好休息。

** delay 〔dɪ'le〕 *n*. 耽擱　　**deliver** 〔dɪ'lɪvɚ〕 *v*. 遞送　　**sign** 〔saɪn〕 *v*. 簽字

6 送錯行李時
Delivery to the Wrong Room

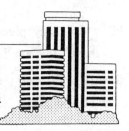

╭─ 〆 **對話精華** 〆 ─────────╮

◈ Is there a name tag attached to them?
上面有沒有繫上姓名的籤條?

◈ I'll check immediately and call you back.
我立刻檢查並給您回電。

╰──────────────────────╯

Dialogue: *BC* = **Bell Captain** 旅館服務生領班 *G* = **Guest** 旅客

BC: This is the Bell Captain's Desk. May I help you?

G : Yes, I've been waiting for my bags *to be sent up for the last half hour*. Where are they?

BC: I'm very sorry to hear that, ma'am. *May I have your name and room number*, please?

G : Yes, it's Brandeis. Room #2312.

BC:服務台,能為您效勞嗎?

G :是這樣的,我等行李送上來至少等了半個小時,行李哪裡去了?

BC:女士,非常抱歉,可以請問您的芳名及房間號碼嗎?

G :好的,我是2312號房的布蘭黛絲。

BC: How many pieces did you have, ma'am?

BC: 女士，您有多少件行李？

G : Two suitcases and a shoulder bag.

G : 兩個旅行箱和一個手提包。

BC: *Could you describe them*, please?

BC: 請描述一下好嗎？

G : The suitcases are *pale* blue leather and the shoulder bag is *dark* brown.

G : 旅行箱是淺藍色皮質的，手提包是深咖啡色的。

BC: *Is there a name tag attached to them*, ma'am?

BC: 上面有沒有繫上姓名的籤條？

G : Yes, they all have tags on them.

G : 有的，每一件都有籤條。

BC: We're very sorry for the delay, ma'am. *I'll check immediately and call you back.*

BC: 女士，對不起，耽擱了您的時間，我立刻檢查並給您回電。

BC: This is the *Bell Captain*. Your bags are *on the way* now. We're very sorry *for the inconvenience*.

BC: 我是服務生領班。您的行李正給您送過去。很抱歉給您帶來不便。

G : How long will it take him?

G : 還需要多久？

BC: About five minutes, ma'am ?

G : I see, all right. Thank you. Bye !

BC: Goodbye, ma'am.

BC: 大約五分鐘，女士。

G : 哦，好。謝謝你，再見！

BC: 再見，女士。

** **sign** 〔saɪn〕 *v.* 簽字
   shoulder bag 有肩帶的女用手提包
   describe 〔dɪ'skraɪb〕 *v.* 描述；說明
   leather 〔'lɛðɚ〕 *n.* 皮革
   attach 〔ə'tætʃ〕 *v.* 繫
   immediately 〔ɪ'midɪɪtlɪ〕 *adv.* 立即
   inconvenience 〔ˌɪnkən'vinjəns〕 *n.* 不便

7 回應客人的召喚
Answering Calls

《 對話精華 》

◎ How much will the cable be ? 這封電報要多少錢 ?

◎ Sorry, I can't say. We'll let you know later.
抱歉，我不知道，稍後再告訴您。

Dialogue： *B* = **Bellman** (爲旅客搬送行李的) 服務生　*G* = **Guest** 旅客

B ： (*knocks at the door*)

G ： Come in. Will you have these cable and letters sent ? How much will they be ?

B ： *Sorry, I can't say. We'll let you know later.*

G ： Well, never mind. Just have them charged. I want to send this box to Stateside. You get me some wrapping paper and cord.

B ： (敲門)

G ： 請進，幫我郵寄電報和信件好嗎 ? 總共要多少錢 ?

B ： 抱歉，我不知道，稍後再告訴您。

G ： 哦，沒關係。就讓它們記帳好了。我要把這個盒子寄回美國，你幫我找些包裝紙和繩子來。

B : Yes, madam... ***Will these do***?

B：是的，女士。…這些可以嗎？

G : Let me see them... I'm afraid this paper isn't quite large enough.

G：讓我看看…這張紙恐怕不夠大。

B : I see. ***I'll find something better***.

B：哦，我再找更好的來。

G : That looks better. Now, ***will you do this up for me***?

G：那張看起來好多了。你幫我把這個弄上來好嗎？

B : Yes... Is this all right?

B：好的…這樣可以嗎？

G : That looks fine. ***You did a good job of it***. Thank you.

G：看起來不錯。你做得很好，謝謝。

B : You are quite welcome.

B：不客氣。

G : Now I have to put down the address. Do you have anything that will write bold?

G：現在我必須寫上地址，你有沒有可以寫粗體字的筆？

B : Yes, ***I'll get the magic ink***. ***That ought to do***.

B：有，我去拿奇異筆。那應該可以。

G : That's just the thing I need. You'll see... There!

G：這就是我要的東西。你看…就是這樣。

** **stateside** 〔'stet,saɪd〕*n*. 美國本土　**wrapping** 〔'ræpɪŋ〕*n*. 包裝紙、布等
cord 〔kɔrd〕*n*. 細繩　　**address** 〔ə'drɛs〕*n*. 住址
bold 〔bold〕*adj*. 粗體字的；顯目的　　***magic ink*** 奇異筆

退宿時拿行李下樓
Bringing Baggage down

∥ 對話精華 ∥

⊛ Could you *pick up* my luggage, please？
請來幫我拿行李好嗎？

⊛ This is your *claim tag*, sir. 這是您的取物條,先生。

Dialogue: *BC* = **Bell Captain** 服務生的領班　*G* = **Guest** 旅客
B = **Bellman** (為旅客搬送行李的) 服務生

BC: This is the Bell Captain's Desk. May I help you?

BC: 服務台,能為您效勞嗎?

G : I'm going to *check out* soon. Could you *pick up* my luggage, please?

G : 我馬上要退宿,請來幫我拿行李好嗎?

BC: Certainly, sir. *May I have your room number*, please?

BC: 好的,先生。請告訴我您的房間號碼好嗎?

G : Yes, it's 2932.

G : 好的,2932號房。

BC: Room #2932. We will send a bellman immediately. *Could you wait in your room*, please?

BC: 2932號房,我立刻派服務生過去,請在房間等候好嗎?

B : Good morning, sir. *I've come for your bags*.

B：先生，早安。我來取您的行李。

G : Thank you. Could you take these two suitcases, please? I'll *bring* the shoulder bag *with* me.

G：謝謝。你拿這兩個旅行箱好嗎？我自己帶著手提包。

B : Certainly, sir. Two suitcases ?

B：當然好，先生。兩個旅行箱嗎？

G : Yes.

G：是的。

B : Is there anything valuable or breakable in them ?

B：裏面有什麼貴重或易碎物品嗎？

G : No.

G：沒有。

B : *This is your claim tag*, sir. We will *keep* your bags *at* the Bell Captain's Desk. *Could you pick them up there*, please ?

B：這是您的取物條。我們會將您的行李存放在服務台。請到那兒領取好嗎？

G : Certainly.

G：好的。

B : Thank you, sir.

B：謝謝您，先生。

▌ 活 用 練 習 ▐

1. Your bags will be at the Bell Captain's Desk.
   您的行李將放在服務台。

2. Your bags will be *kept* at the Bell Captain's Desk.
   您的行李將存放在服務台。

3. *Your bags may be picked up from* the Bell Captain's Desk.
   您可以到服務台領取行李。

4. Could you *come down* to the Bell Captain's Desk with your
   claim tag to *pick up* your bags, sir?
   先生，請帶著取物條到樓下服務台領取行李好嗎？

5. Please pick up（*ask for*）a *long-term storage tag* at the
   Bell Captain's Desk.
   請到服務台領取長期存物證。

6. I'm afraid we cannot *be responsible for* any damage
   （*breakage, spillage, spoilage*）.
   任何損壞（破損、滲漏、腐敗）我們恐怕都不負責。

** *check out* "結帳退宿"   *pick up* "拿起；舉起"
    claim tag 取物條
    long term storage tag 長期寄物證
    be responsible for "對…負責"
    spillage〔'spɪlɪdʒ〕*n*. 滲漏；溢出
    spoilage〔'spɔɪlɪdʒ〕*n*. 腐敗；損壞

客人要求提取行李時
Picking up the Guest's Bags

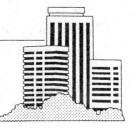

∫ **對話精華** ∫

◬ What time will you be *checking out* ?
　您什麼時候要結帳？

◬ Could you *make sure* that your bags are packed before you leave ?
　請您在離開前確定行李打包好了沒？

◬ I hope you have *enjoyed your stay*.
　但願您停留期間一切還愉快。

Dialogue: *G* = Guest 旅客　　*BC* = Bell Captain 服務生領班

G : Hello. Is this the Bell Captain's Desk ?

G：喂，是服務台嗎？

BC: *Speaking*. May I help you?

BC：是的，能爲您效勞嗎？

G : Yes. I'll be checking out in about an hour but I'd like to *have lunch* before then. *Could you arrange to have my bags brought down* while I'm out ?

G：我再過一個小時左右要結帳，但結帳之前，我想先去吃午飯。我出去時，您是否可以安排把我的行李運下來呢？

BC: Certainly, sir. May I have your room number, please?

好的，先生。請告訴我您的房間號碼好嗎？

G : #2824.

2824室。

BC: What time will you be checking out ?

您什麼時候要結帳？

G : Around 11:30 a.m.

大約早上11點半。

BC: I see, sir. Could you make sure that your bags are packed before you leave ?

我知道了，先生請您在離開前確定行李打包好了沒？

G : Sure.

好的。

BC: You may *collect* your bags *from* the Bell Captain's Desk in the Lobby. I hope you have *enjoyed your stay.*

您可以在大廳的服務台領取行李，但願您停留期間一切還愉快。

** *speaking* 電話用語，意指「我就是」，相當於 *This is he speaking.*
lobby〔ˈlɑbɪ〕*n*. 旅館大廳

10

領取行李時
Collecting One's Bags

〞**對話精華** 〞

▲ May I see *your room key*, please?
請把房間鑰匙拿給我看好嗎?

▲ May I see *some identification*, please?
請讓我看看身分證明好嗎?

Dialogue: *G* = **Guest** 旅客   *BC* = **Bell Captain** 服務生領班

G : I asked for my bags to be
picked up from my room.
Do you have them?

G : 我要求到我房間取行李,你
們拿來了嗎?

BC: Certainly, sir. *May I see
your room key*, please?

BC: 當然,先生。請把房間鑰匙
拿給我看,好嗎?

G : I don't have it. I've already checked out.

G : 我沒有鑰匙。我已經結帳退
宿了。

BC: I see. *May I see your
final bill then*, sir?

BC: 我知道了。先生,那麼我可
以看看您的收據嗎?

G : Sure, here you are.

G : 當然可以,在這兒。

BC: Thank you, sir. A bellman will bring your **bags**. Just a moment, please.

BC: 先生，謝謝，服務生會把您的行李送過來，請稍等。

** *final bill* 收據；帳單

identification 〔aɪ͵dɛntəfəˈkeʃən〕 *n*. 證件；身份證明

11

寄存物品時
Depositing Some Items

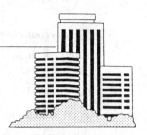

~ *對話精華* ~

◭ I'd like to *leave* this *with* you.
我想把這個寄放在你這兒。

◭ This cloakroom *is open until* 9 p.m.
本寄物處開放到下午九點。

◭ You may *collect* it there.
您可以去那兒領取。

Dialogue: *G* = Guest 旅客　　**Bellman**（爲旅客搬送行李的）服務生

G : I'd like to *leave* this *with* you.

G : 我想把這個寄放在你這兒。

B : Certainly, ma'am. Is there anything *valuable* or *breakable* in your bag?

B : 好的，女士，請問袋子裏有沒有貴重或易碎物品？

G : No.

G : 沒有。

B : Thank you. Here is your tag #33.

B : 謝謝。這是您的33號取物牌。

G : When does the cloakroom close?

G : 寄物處幾點關門？

B : *This cloakroom is open until 9 p.m.*

B：本寄物處開放到下午 9 點。

G : *Oh, dear* ! I won't be back until about 10:30 tonight. Where can I pick up my bag ?

G：糟糕！我今晚10點半左右才會回來。我到哪裡領取袋子呢？

B : *We will transfer your bag to* the Lobby Floor Cloakroom. You may *collect* it there, ma'am.

B：我們會將您的袋子轉交給一樓大廳的寄物處，女士，您可以去那兒領取。

G : I see. Thanks a lot.

G：我知道了，非常謝謝。

B : You're welcome.

B：不客氣。

活 用 練 習

① There are *safety deposit boxes* at the Front Desk.
櫃枱有存放貴重物品的保險櫃。

② Could you leave your suitcase at the Bell Captain's Desk ?
請把手提箱寄放在服務台好嗎？

③ Just a moment, please. I'll call the manager. 請稍等，我叫經理。

④ I'm afraid we cannot accept *perishable* goods here.
我們這裏恐怕不能受理易腐敗的物品。

** **cloakroom** 〔'klok,rum〕 *n.* 寄物處   **transfer** 〔træns'fɝ〕 *v.* 移轉
collect 〔kə'lɛkt〕 *v.* 收回   **deposit** 〔dɪ'pɑzɪt〕 *n.* 保管處
perishable 〔'pɛrɪʃəb!〕 *adj.* 易壞的

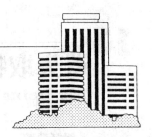

12 領取寄存物品時
Collecting One's Items

∬ **對話精華** ∬

♠ *May I have your tag*, please？
請把取物牌給我好嗎？

♠ Could you check that *everything is here*？
請檢查東西是不是都在呢？

Dialogue: *G* = **Guest** 旅客　*B* = **Bellman**（爲旅客搬送行李的）服務生

G： I *left* my bag *with* you this morning.

B： Certainly, sir. *May I have your tag*, please？

G： Sure. Here you are.

B： Thank you, sir. Just a moment, please.
Thank you for waiting, sir.
Is this everything？

G： Yes, that's all there was. Thanks a lot.

G： You're welcome, sir.

G：我今天早上把袋子寄放在你這裏。

B：好的，先生，請把取物牌給我好嗎？

G：好的，在這兒。

B：謝謝，請稍候。
讓您久等了，先生。東西全都在嗎？

G：是的，就是這些，多謝你。

B：不客氣，先生。

13

遺失取物牌時
Tag Being Lost

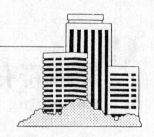

〽對話精華〽

◉ Did you leave it *at this cloakroom*, sir?
先生,您是寄放在本存物處嗎?

◉ *Could you describe* the jacket, please?
請描述一下那件夾克的樣子好嗎?

◉ *Sorry for all the trouble.* 抱歉這樣麻煩你。

Dialogue : *B* = **Bellman** 服務生　*G* = **Guest** 旅客

B : Good afternoon, sir. May I help you?

B : 午安,能為您效勞嗎?

G : Yes, I *left* my jacket *with* you this morning but I've lost the tag for it.

G : 是的,我今天早上把夾克寄放在你這兒,可是我把取物牌弄丟了。

B : I see, sir. Do you remember the tag's number or color?

B : 哦,先生,您記得牌子的號碼或顏色嗎?

G : I'm afraid not. I think it was blue but I'm not sure.

G : 恐怕記不得了。大概是藍色的,但是我不確定。

B : Did you *leave* it *at* this cloakroom, sir?

B : 先生,您是寄放在本存物處嗎?

G : Yes.

G : 是的。

B : Could you describe the
jacket, please?

B : 請您描述一下那件夾克的樣
子好嗎?

G : Yes, it's a *beige corduroy*
jacket with a brown *checked*
lining.

G : 那是件灰褐色的灯心絨夾克,
上面有咖啡色格子花紋線條。

B : Is there anything in the
pockets, sir?

B : 先生,口袋裏有沒有東西?

G : Let's see. There should be
a light blue *handkerchief*, a
key chain and some *business
cards* in the pocket. The *label* says "St. Michael".

G : 我想想看,口袋裏應該有一
條淺藍色的手帕,一個鑰匙
鍊和一些名片。標籤上寫著
"St. Michael"。

B : *Is your name marked on the
jacket*, sir?

B : 先生,夾克上面有沒有標註
您的姓名。

G : No, I don't think so.

G : 不,我想沒有。

B : May I see some *identification*, please?

B : 我可以看一下您的身分證明
嗎?

G : Well, here's my card but
why all the questions?

G : 哦,這是我的名片,你爲什
麼要問這些問題呢?

B : We have many similar
jackets in the cloakroom
and we might *make a mis-
take*.

B : 本存物處有許多件類似的夾
克,我們可能會搞錯。

G : I see.

G : 我懂了。

B : Just a moment, please. I'll check for you. ……
Thank you for waiting, sir. Is this your jacket?

B：請稍等，我幫您查查看。……

讓您久等了，先生，這是您的夾克嗎？

G : That's the one. *Sorry for all the trouble.*

G：就是那件，抱歉這樣麻煩你。

B : *Not at all*, sir. *Have a nice day.*

B：不客氣，先生，祝您愉快。

** **beige** 〔beʒ〕*adj*. 灰褐色的
   corduroy 〔ˏkɔrdəˈrɔɪ〕*n*. 燈心絨
   checked 〔tʃɛkt〕*adj*. 格子花紋的
   handkerchief 〔ˈhæŋkətʃɪf〕*n*. 手帕
   business card 名片
   label 〔ˈlebl̩〕*n*. 標籤

14 門房的應對
Doorman's Service

『 **對話精華** 』

◉ Good evening, sir. Are you *checking in*?
　先生，晚安，您要登記住宿嗎？

◉ Do you have any baggage *in the trunk*?
　有沒有行李放在行李箱裏？

◉ *Is this everything*, sir? 先生，東西全在這兒嗎？

Dialogue：　*D* = **Doorman** 門房　　*G* = **Guest** 旅客

D： Good afternoon, sir. Welcome to the Grand Hotel?

D：先生，午安，歡迎光臨圓山大飯店。

G： Thank you.

G：謝謝。

D： Are you checking in, sir?

D：先生，您要登記住宿嗎？

G： Yes, where is the Front Desk?

G：是的，櫃枱在哪兒？

D： *I'll show you the way*, sir. This way, please.

D：我帶您去，先生，請走這邊。

G： OK.

G：好的。

活 用 練 習

1 May I *help* you *with* your bags, sir？
　先生，我幫您提行李好嗎？

2 *How many bags do you have in all*？您一共有多少件行李？

3 A bellman will show you to the Front Desk.
　服務生會領您到櫃枱去。

4 It's slippery. *Please mind your feet*.　地很滑，請小心走。

5 Please *mind* your head. 小心您的頭。

6 Please *mind* your hands *in the revolving door*.
　過旋轉門時請小心您的手。

7 Please go in by the door on the left. 請從左邊的門進去。

8 *Would you like me to give directions to the taxi driver*？
　要我向計程車司機說明嗎？

9 *Please show this card to the driver* when you return to the
　hotel. 您要回旅館時，請給司機看這張名片。

** trunk〔trʌŋk〕*n.* 汽車尾部的行李箱
　slippery〔'slɪpərɪ〕*adj.* 光滑的
　revolving door 旋轉門

Part 4

訂房專線
Room Reservations

1 來自國內的預約
Reservation from a Domestic Source

〖 對話精華 〗

◉ I'd like to *reserve a room*. 我想預訂一個房間。

◉ *Which date* would that be? 要訂在什麼時候？

◉ *How many nights* do you wish to stay？ 您希望住幾晚？

Dialogue: *C* = **Clerk** 櫃枱職員　*G* = **Guest** 旅客

C : Good morning. This is Room Reservations. May I help you, sir?

C : 客房預約部，您早，能爲您效勞嗎？

G : Yes, I'd like to *reserve a room*.

G : 我想預訂一個房間。

C : Thank you, sir. *For which date* ?

C : 謝謝您，要訂在什麼時候？

G : From October 15th.

G : 從 10 月 15 號開始。

C : *For how many nights*?

C : 要住幾晚呢？

G : For three nights.

G : 三個晚上。

C : *How many guests will there be in your party*?

C : 您一行共有多少位客人呢？

G : Just my wife and myself.

G：只有我太太和我。

C : Which kind of room would you prefer, *a double or a twin*?

C：您喜歡什麼樣的房間，要一張雙人床或兩張單人床的房間呢？

G : A twin please.

G：請給我一間兩張單人床的房間。

C : Could you *hold the line*, please? *I'll check our room availability for those days*. Thank you for waiting, sir. We have a twin at NT\$1,000 and at NT\$1,500. Which would you prefer?

C：請別掛斷好嗎？我要查查那幾天有沒有空房間。先生，讓你久等了，我們有台幣1,000元和1,500元的雙人房，您喜歡哪一種？

G : We'll take the one at NT\$1,500.

G：我們要訂1,500元的那一種。

C : Certainly, sir. May I have your name and *initials*, please?

C：好的，先生，請告訴我您貴姓及名字的第一個字母好嗎？

G : Yes, it's Carruthers T.E.

G：好的，我叫凱魯瑟斯T.E.。

C : *How do you spell that*, please?

C：請告訴我怎麼拼好嗎？

G : C, A, double R, U, T, H, E, R, S.

G：C，A兩個R，U，T，H，E，R，S。

C : Mr. Carruthers. May I have your phone number, please?

G : Yes, the number is 06-321-2345.

C : 06-321-2345. *Is this your home phone number*?

G : Yes, it is.

C : What time do you expect to arrive, sir?

G : Oh, around 6 p.m, I suppose.

C : *I'd like to confirm your reservation*. A twin room for Mr. and Mrs. Carruthers at NT$1,500, per night for three nights from October 15th to October 17th. My name is Steve and *we look forward to serving you*.

C : 凱魯瑟斯先生，請給我您的電話號碼好嗎？

G : 好的，號碼是06-321-2345。

C : 06-321-2345. 這是您府上的電話號碼嗎？

G : 是的。

C : 先生，您預定什麼時候抵達？

G : 嗯，我想是下午六點左右吧。

C : 我要再確定一下您的預約。凱魯瑟斯夫婦要一間兩張床的雙人房，每晚1,500元。從10月15號到17號三晚，我叫史迪夫，期待能為您服務。

** *room reservation* 客房預約部　 reserve 〔rɪ'zɜv〕 *v*. 預訂
double 〔'dʌbḷ〕 *n*. 一張雙人床的房間　 twin 〔twɪn〕 *n*. 兩張單人床的雙人房
availability 〔ə͵velə'bɪlətɪ〕 *n*. 可用　 initial 〔ɪ'nɪʃəl〕 *n*. 姓名的起首字母
look forward to + Ving "期待"

由第三者預約時
Reservation Made by a Third Party

∥ 對話精華 ∥

▲ Which kind of room *would they prefer*?
他們比較喜歡什麼樣的房間?

▲ *To* whom should we *send the bill*? 我們應該把帳單寄給誰?

▲ Would you like us to *charge this to your company*?
您要我們向貴公司索費嗎?

Dialogue: *C* = Clerk 櫃枱職員　　*G* = Guest 旅客

C : Good morning. Room Reservations. May I help you, sir?

C : 客房預約部,您早,能為您效勞嗎?

G : Yes, I'd like to *reserve* a room *for* a *colleague*.

G : 我想替一位同事預訂房間。

C : Thank you, sir. **Which date would that be?**

C : 謝謝您,先生。要訂什麼時候?

G : For one week. From November 1 to 7.

G : 從11月1日到7日,總共一個星期。

C : Which kind of room would they prefer?

C : 他們比較喜歡什麼樣的房間?

G : A double. He'll *be accom-panied by* his wife.

G：一間雙人床的房間，他太太要陪他來。

C : Could you *hold the line*, please? I'll check our room availability.……
Thank you for waiting. I'm afraid we have no double rooms, *but we do have some twin rooms at* NT$1,000 *and* NT$1,500 *available*.

C：請別掛斷好嗎？我查查是否有房間可用。……讓您久等了。我們恐怕沒有雙人床的房間，但是我們還有幾間價位 1,000元及 1,500元台幣的兩張單人床房間。

G : The one at NT$1,500 sounds fine.

G：1,500元的那種聽起來挺不錯。

C : Certainly, sir. May we know the name of your colleague and his wife?

C：好的，能告訴我你同事夫婦貴姓嗎？

G : Mr. and Mrs. Vernon Williams.

G：華儂·威廉斯夫婦。

C : Thank you. May I have your name and telephone number, please?

C：謝謝，請告訴我您的姓名和電話號碼好嗎？

G : Yes, it's 585-2311, ex-tension 1201. I *work in* IBM Taiwan Corp. My name is Dan Smith.

G：好的，585-2311,轉1201。我在台灣國際商業機器公司工作，我叫丹·史密斯。

C : We do *offer special rates* for your company, sir. For a twin room there is a 10% *discount*. Shall we charge this to your colleague directly?

C : 本店提供特價給貴公司，雙人房打九折。我們是直接向您的同事收費嗎？

G : To my company, please.

G : 請向敝公司收費。

C : Which department should the bill be *made out* to?

C : 這份帳單應該送到哪個部門？

G : To the *Accounting Department*, please.

G : 請寄到會計部。

C : Do you know their *flight number* and *arrival time*?

C : 您曉得他們的班機號碼和抵達時間嗎？

G : Yes, it's Pan American Flight #412. His flight arrives at 3 p.m., so he should be there by 6 p.m. *at the earliest*.

G : 是的，是泛美航空412班機。他的班機下午三點抵達，所以他應該最早下午六點到貴店。

C : Thank you very much. My name is Johnson. If you have any further enquiries, please *don't hesitate* to contact me. We *look forward* to serving your colleague.

C : 謝謝，我叫強生，如果您想進一步詢問的話，請不要猶豫儘管和我聯絡。我們期待能為您的同事服務。

◎ 活 用 練 習 ◎

[1] A single room is NT$1000 per night. There is also a 10% *tax* and a 10% *service charge*.

單人房每晚 1000 元，另外還要加算 10% 的稅金和 10% 的服務費。

[2] I'm afraid we have no *credit arrangements* with your company. We will need an *advance deposit* by *bank draft* or *in cash* before the reservation date.

恐怕我們和貴公司沒有信用貸款的協定，您必須在預約日之前，預先送來銀行滙票或現金，做爲訂金。

** colleague〔ˈkɑlig〕*n.* 同事
 be accompanied by 由…陪同
 special rate 特價
 discount〔ˈdɪskaʊnt〕*n.* 折扣
 Accounting Department 會計部門
 hesitate〔ˈhɛzə,tet〕*v.* 猶豫
 tax〔tæks〕*n.* 稅金
 credit arrangements 信貸協定
 bank draft 銀行滙票

3

來自國外的預約
Reservation from Overseas

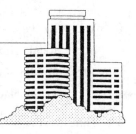

〔 *對話精華* 〕

🔺 May I have your *airline* and *flight number*, please？
請問您搭乘哪一家航空公司及班機號碼？

🔺 Where can we *contact* you in Taiwan？
在台灣我們可以經由哪個單位與您聯絡？

Dialogue： *C* = **Clerk** 櫃枱職員　　*G* = **Guest** 旅客

（ *confirms arrival date time* ）

（確認抵達日期和時間）

C： May I have your airline and flight number, please?

G： Pan Am Flight #002 *departing from* New York on May 8th.

C： Do you know your *arrival time* at Chiang Kai-Shek Airport, sir?

G： Yes, it's. 3 p.m. *local time*.

C：請告訴我您搭乘的航空公司及班機號碼好嗎？

G：5月8號由紐約起飛的泛美002班機。

C：先生，您知道您抵達中正國際機場的時間嗎？

G：知道，當地時間下午三點。

C : You will be arriving at 3 p.m. local time on May 10th on Pan Am Flight #002 from New York?

G : That's it.

C : Where can we contact you in Taiwan?

G : Well, *care of* my Taiwanese agent, Lihwan Trading Company. The number is （06）203-6851.

C : 203-6851. Thank you, sir; We look forward to serving you. *Have a safe trip.*

C : 您預定搭乘由紐約起飛的泛美002班機，於5月10日本地時間下午3點到達。

G : 就是這樣。

C : 在台灣我們可以經由哪個單位與您聯絡？

G : 哦，可以由我的台灣代理商麗華貿易公司轉告給我。電話號碼是（06）203-6851。

C : 203-6851。謝謝您，先生。我們期待能為您服務，祝您旅途平安。

＊＊ depart〔dɪˈpɑrt〕v. 起飛

想要的客房没有空缺時
Desired Room Being Unavailable

對話精華

◉ Which kind of room would you prefer？
  您喜歡什麼樣的房間？

◉ *A double room*, please. 請給我一間雙人房。

◉ I'm afraid we *have no double rooms available*, but we can offer you a twin room.
  我們恐怕沒有雙人床的房間了，但是可以提供您兩張單人床的房間。

Dialogue: *C* = Clerk 櫃枱職員　*G* = Guest 旅客

C : Which kind of room *would* you *prefer*?

C：您喜歡什麼樣的房間？

G : A double room, please.

G：請給我一間雙人床。

C : Could you *hold the line*, please? I'll check our room availability for those days.

C：請別掛斷好嗎？我要查查那幾天的空房間。

Thank you for waiting. I'm afraid we have no double rooms *available* but we can offer you a twin room.

讓您久等了。我們恐怕沒有雙人床的房間了，但是可以提供您兩張單人床的房間。

G : I see. How much will that be?

G : 哦，價錢多少？

C : We have a twin at NT$1000 and at NT$1,500. Which *would* you *prefer*?

C : 我們有台幣1,000元和1,500元的兩張單人床房間，您喜歡哪一種？

G : I'll take the one at NT $1,000.

G : 我訂1,000元的那一種。

C : Thank you, sir.

C : 謝謝您，先生。

5

旅館客滿時
When the Hotel Is Full

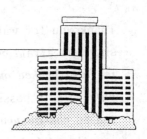

~ *∥ 對話精華 ∥* ~

♠ I'm sorry but *we are all booked for* next week.
抱歉，下個星期的房間都被訂光了。

♠ Is it possible for you to *change your reservation date*?
您可不可以改變預約日期呢？

Dialogue: *C* = **Clerk** 櫃枱職員   *G* = **Guest** 旅客

C : Good morning. Room Reservations. May I help you, sir?

C : 客房預約部，您早，能為您效勞嗎？

G : I'd like to *make a reservation.*

G : 我想預訂房間。

C : Which date would that be?

C : 要訂在什麼時候？

G : For the night of April 18th for one night.

G : 訂 4 月18號一個晚上。

C : Could you hold the line, please? I'll check our room availability for that day. ……

C : 請別掛斷？我要檢查一下那天的空房間。……

Thank you for waiting, sir. I'm afraid *our hotel is fully booked on that night*. Is it possible for you to *change your reservation date*?

讓您久等了，先生。本店那晚的房間恐怕已經登記額滿，您可不可以改變預約日期呢？

G : No, that's not possible.

G：不，不可能。

C : *We might have cancellations*. Could you call us again closer to the date?

C：或許有人會取消預約，請您接近那個日期時再打電話來好嗎？

G : Sure, but if you do have any cancellations, could you let me know as soon as possible?

G：好的，如果眞有人取消，能不能儘快讓我知道呢？

C : I'm very sorry, sir, but we are unable to do that. We would *appreciate* it very much *if you could call us instead*.

C：先生，非常抱歉，我們不能那樣做，如果改由您打電話來，我們將會非常感激。

G : Well, if that's the case…

G：哦，如果是這樣……

C : We're very sorry, sir. *We hope you understand*.

C：先生，非常抱歉，希望您能諒解。

◉ 活 用 練 習 ◉

1 This is the busiest season. I'm very sorry but could you *call us again later on this week*? We may have a cancellation.

現在是旺季。非常抱歉，但是能不能請您這個週末再打電話過來？可能會有人取消預約。

** cancellation 〔,kænsḷˈleʃən〕 *n.* 取消
appreciate 〔əˈpriʃɪ,et〕 *v.* 感激

6

無法連續預約至期滿
Can't Be Booked for All the Nights Requested

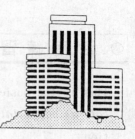

〰 *對話精華* 〰

🔻 We *are fully booked for* all types of rooms on that night.
那天晚上各種類型的房間都預約額滿了。

🔻 Can you *book* me *into* another hotel in the area?
可不可以替我在當地預訂另一家旅館呢？

Dialogue: *C* = **Clerk** 櫃枱職員　　*G* = **Guest** 旅客

C : Good morning. Room Reservations. May I help
you, sir?

C : 早安，客房預約部，能為您
效勞嗎？

G : Yes, I'd like to *reserve
a room*.

G : 是的，我想預訂一個房間。

C : Which date would that be?

C : 要訂什麼時候的？

G : I'd like a twin room for
6 nights from May 15th.

G : 從5月15日起六個晚上，我
要一間有兩張單人床的房間。

C : Could you *hold the line*,
please? I'll check our
room availability for those
days. ……

C : 您請稍等好嗎？我查一下那
幾天的空房間。……

Thank you for waiting, sir. *We have a twin available for* four nights from May 15th and also for May 20th, but I'm afraid *there is none available on the night of* May 19th.

先生，讓您久等了，我們在5月15日到18日四天以及20日都有兩張單人床的空房間，可是5月19號沒有。

G : Well, do you have two singles for that night?

G : 那麼，那天晚上有沒有兩間單人房呢？

C : I'm very sorry, sir, but *we are fully booked for all types of rooms* on that night.

C : 非常抱歉，那天晚上所有類型的客房都預約額滿了。

G : I see. Can you *book* me *into* another hotel in the area?

G : 哦，可不可以替我在當地預訂另一家旅館呢？

C : I'm afraid *we don't have any information on their room availability*. Would you like me to book you for all nights *except* the 19th?

C : 我們恐怕沒有他們空房間的資料。要我幫您登記19號以外的晚上的房間嗎？

G : I'll think about it and let you know.

G : 我考慮一下再通知你。

C : Thank you, sir. We look forward to *hearing from* you.

C：謝謝您，先生，我們期待您的消息。

◎ 活 用 練 習 ◎

1 I must *apologize for* the *inconvenience*.

我必須爲此不便向您致歉。

7

提供差一等的客房
A Lower Quality Is Offered

~~~ 〚對話精華〛 ~~~

◉ We don't have any single *available*.

　我們沒有任何空的單人房。

◉ Would you mind a double room *instead*?

　您介意改住雙人房嗎？

Dialogue: *C* = **Clerk** 櫃枱職員　　*G* = **Guest** 旅客

C : Which kind of room would you prefer?

C : 您喜歡什麼樣的房間？

G : I was in a twin room for single use last time. The same type will be fine.

G : 我上次一個人住有兩張床的雙人房，那種房間不錯。

C : I'm very sorry, sir, but I'm afraid no twin rooms are available on that day. *Would you mind a smaller single room at* NT$ 1,000 *instead*?

C : 抱歉，那天恐怕沒有空的雙人房。您介意改用較小的 1,000元單人房嗎？

G : Yes, that's all right.

G : 好的，沒有關係。

C : Thank you, sir.

C : 謝謝您，先生。

詢問對房間視野的喜好
Room View

〖 對話精華 〗

◉ Which kind of room would you prefer？您喜歡哪一種房間？

◉ I'd like a room *with* a sea view (*mountain view*).
我要一間看得見海景（山景）的房間。

Dialogue: *C* = **Clerk** 櫃枱職員　　*G* = **Guest** 旅客

C : *Which kind of room would you prefer*?

C : 您喜歡哪一種房間？

G : A twin, please.

G : 請給我一間兩張床的雙人房。

C : We have a twin at NT $1,000 per night.

C : 我們有一晚台幣 1,000 元的雙人房。

G : I'd like a quiet room *with a view of* Yangmingshan, please.

G : 我要一間看得到陽明山的雅房。

C : I see, sir. We will *do our best*.

C : 我曉得了，先生。我們會盡力安排。

G : Thanks a lot.

G : 非常謝謝。

C : You're welcome, sir.

C : 不客氣。

9

詢問對房間類型的喜好
Room Type

〃 **對話精華** 〃

🔺 We'll note down your request and *if two twin rooms with a connecting door become available*, we'll reserve them for you.

我們會記下您的要求，若有中門隔開的兩間雙人房，我們會為您保留。

Dialogue: *C* = **Clerk** 櫃枱職員　　*G* = **Guest** 旅客

C : Which kind of room would you prefer?

C : 您喜歡哪一種房間？

G : We're a family of four. I'd prefer connecting rooms if possible.

G : 我們一家四個人，可能的話我喜歡以門相隔的房間。

C : We will do our best to *book you into connecting rooms*. If this is not possible, *would you mind adjoining rooms, instead*?

C : 我們會盡力替您登記相連的房間。如果沒辦法，您介不介意以相鄰接的房間代替呢？

G: No, but we'd really prefer connecting ones as the children are small.

G: 不介意，但是因為孩子們年紀小，我們非常希望以門相隔的房間。

** sea view 海景　　mountain view 山景

with a view 看得見　　*do one's best* 盡力

connecting room 以門相隔的房間

adjoining room 相鄰接的房間

10 床位大小及數目
Bed-size & Number in Room

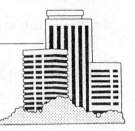

〚**對話精華**〛

◉ I'm rather tall and I'd like a room *with a very large bed*.

我很高，我想要一間有大床的房間。

◉ Certainly, sir. *We'll book you into the room with a king-size bed*.

好的，先生。我們會替您登記一間有特大號床的房間。

Dialogue: *C* = **Clerk** 櫃枱職員　　*G* = **Guest** 旅客

C : Which kind of room would you prefer?

C : 您喜歡哪一種房間？

G : One for myself, my wife and my son. We'd all like to be in the same room.

G : 一間供我、我太太和我兒子住的房間。我們都喜歡住在同一個房間。

C : I'm afraid we have no *triple rooms* but we can *put an extra bed into one of our double rooms.* Would that suit you?

C : 我們恐怕沒有三人房了，但是我們可以另加一張床在雙人房裏，這樣合適嗎？

G：Yes，that's fine.   G：好的，那樣很好。

** triple〔'trɪpḷ〕*adj.* 三倍的   extra〔'ɛkstrə〕*adj.* 特加的
king-size 特大號

11 確認預約的電話
Confirmation Call

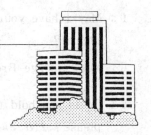

〴 對話精華 〵

● I'd like to *confirm a reservation.* 我要確認一項預約。

● We have no record of a reservation (*for that date*) *in your room.* 我們沒有您（當天）的預約記錄。

● What was the date of the reservation? 您是什麼時候預約的？

Dialogue: *C* = Clerk 櫃枱職員　　*G* = Guest 旅客

C : Good morning. This is Room Reservations. May I help you, sir?

C : 客房預約部，您早，能為您效勞嗎？

G : Yes, I'd like to *confirm a reservation.*

G : 我要確認一項預約。

C : Certainly, sir. *May I have the date of your reservation*, please?

C : 好的，先生，請告訴我您預約的日期好嗎？

G : It was for April 21st, for one night.

G : 4月21日一個晚上。

C : May I have your name, please?

C : 請問大名好嗎?

G : Yes, George Brown.

G : 好的,喬治布朗。

C : Could you hold the line, please? *I'll check our reservation record.* ······ Thank you for waiting, sir. *Your room is confirmed for that day.* We look forward to serving you.

C : 請稍等,別掛斷電話,我要查查預約記錄。······讓您久等了,先生。您那天的房間確定了。我們期待為您服務。

◉ 活 用 練 習 ◉

1 When did you make the reservation? 您什麼時候預約的?

2 When was the reservation made? 什麼時候預約的?

3 Shall I make a reservation for you? 要我為您預約嗎?

4 *Is this a new reservation or a confirmation call?* 這是新的預約電話還是確認的電話呢?

5 Do you have a reservation or do you wish to make one? 您已經預約了還是想預約呢?

6 Do you remember the name of the reservation clerk? 您記得那位預約員的名字嗎?

⑦ Do you remember the name of the clerk *who accepted the reservation*?

您記得受理這項預約的職員的姓名嗎？

⑧ *In whose name was the reservation made*?

這項預約是用誰的名字訂的？

⑨ The room may have been reserved *in the name of* the person who made the reservation.

這個房間可能已經以辦理此預訂的人之名訂下了。

　＊＊ *hold the line* "別掛斷電話"

　　record〔'rɛkəd〕*n*. 記錄

　　reservation clerk　受理預約的職員

　　in the name of　以⋯名義

12 變更預訂的日期
Change of Reservation Date

~ 〞 對話精華 〞 ~

◉ I'd like to *extend* it for *two more* nights.
我想再延長兩個晚上。

◉ We'll *extend the reservation* for you.
我們會為您延長預約的。

Dialogue: *C* = Clerk 櫃枱職員   *G* = Guest 旅客

C : Room Reservations. May I help you, sir?

C : 客房預約部，能為您效勞嗎?

G : Yes, my name is Athos, and I made a reservation for 3 nights from March 5th. I'd like to *extend it for two more nights until the* 9th.

G : 我叫亞瑟斯，我預訂了從3月5號起三個晚上的房間，我想再延長兩個晚上一直到9號。

C : For 5 nights *from* March 5th *until* March 9th.

C : 從3月5日到3月9日五個晚上。

G : That's right.

G : 對。

C : Will there be any change
   in your room type? Your
   reservation is for a twin
   room.

C : 要不要更改房間的種類呢？
   您所預訂的是兩張床的雙
   人房。

G : No.

G : 不改。

C : Thank you, sir. We will
   extend the reservation
   (*make the cancellation /
   the correction / the
   change*) for you.

C : 謝謝您，我們會為您延長
   （取消/改正/變更）。

** **extend** 〔ɪk'stɛnd〕 *v*. 延長
   correction 〔kə'rɛkʃən〕 *n*. 改正

櫃台 (FRONT DESK)

13

由第三者取消預約時
Cancellation by a Third Party

~~~
∥對話精華∥
~~~

◎ I'd like to *cancel a reservation*. 我要取消一項預約。

◎ *In whose name* was the reservation made?
　　那是以誰的名字預約的？

Dialogue: *C* = **Clerk** 櫃枱職員　　*G* = **Guest** 旅客

C : Room Reservations. May I help you, sir?

C : 客房預約部，能為您效勞嗎？

G : I'd like to cancel a reservation.

G : 我要取消一項預約。

C : *In whose name was the reservation made*?

C : 那是以誰的名字預約的？

G : Claude Rigell.

G : 克勞得・雷傑爾。

C : How do you spell that, please?

C : 請問怎麼拼？

G : R. I. G. E. double L.

G : R、I、G、E、兩個 L。

C : What was the date of the reservation?

C : 什麼時候預約的？

G : From February 27 for 3 nights.

G：從2月27日起三晚。

C : Excuse me, but *is the reservation for yourself or for another party*?

C：對不起，這項預約是爲您自己訂的還是爲別人訂的？

G : It's for my boss.

G：是爲我的老闆訂的。

C : May I have your name and phone number, please?

C：請告訴我您的姓名及電話號碼，好嗎？

G : Yes, it's Christiane Fabre and my number is 245-3971.

G：好的，我叫克麗斯汀‧阿諾法布蕾，電話是245-3971。

C : Thank you, ma'am. I will *cancel* Mr. Rigell's reservation from February 27th for 3 nights. My name is Johnson and *we look forward to another chance to serve you*.

C：謝謝您，女士，我會取消雷傑爾先生自2月27日起三晚的預約。我叫強生，我們期待另有機會爲您服務。

◎ 活 用 練 習 ◎

① We hope we'll *have another opportunity of serving you*.
我們希望另有機會爲您效勞。

** *look forward to* " 期待；盼望 "
opportunity 〔͵ɑpɚˈtjunətɪ 〕 *n*. 機會

住客帳卡

	N 姓 A M E 名						
Room No 序　號	LAST	FIRST	INITIAL	Rate 序　租	Out Date		TAIPEI HILTON ROOM No.
No. of Persons					In Date		
Receptionist					R	NR	CR	Date
TELEPHONE A _____ FROM FOLIO _____ METER　　D _____ TO FOLIO _____							LUGGAGE CHECK

台北希爾頓大飯店
TAIPEI HILTON
台北市忠孝西路一段 38 號
38, CHUNG SIAO W. RD. SEC.1
TAIPEI, REPUBLIC OF CHINA
TEL ：311-5151(40 LINES
CABLE: HIL TELS TAIPEI
TELEX: 11699-HIL TELS

A № 143897

MEMO		DATE 日　期	REFERENCE 摘　　　要	DEBIT 借　方	CREDIT 貸　方	BALANCE 餘　　額	
	1						
	2						
	3						
	4						
	5						
	6						
	7						
	8						
	9						
	10						
	11						
	12						
	13						
	14						
	15						
	16						
	17						
	18						
	19						
	20						
	21						
	22						
	23						
	24						

ABBREVIATIONS 說　明

ROOM	= ROOM CHARGE	房　　租	
SERV	= SERVICE CHARGE	服　務　費	
RESTR	= RESTAURANT	餐　飲　費	
L. DIST	= LONG DISTANCE CALL	長途電話費	
LNDRY	= LAUNDRY	洗　衣　費	
MISC.	= MISCELLANEOUS	什　　費	
TR. CH.	= TRANSFER CHARGE	轉　費　入	
TR. CR.	= TRANSFER CREDIT	轉　費　出	
ADJ.	= ADJUSTMENT	調　整　支	
PD. OUT	= PAID OUT	代　　支	
PAID	= PAID	付　　現	

GUEST SIGNATURE　　顧客簽認

CHARGE TO
付　款　人 _____
ADDRESS
地　　址 _____
APPROVED BY
帳　　准 _____

A
PLEASE HAND
THIS SLIP TO
BELL BOY FOR
YOUR LUGGAGE

№ 143897

Part 5

櫃枱（入宿登記）
The Front Desk (Check-in)

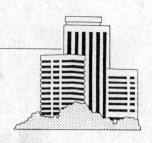

1 入宿登記手續
Check-in Procedure

〖對話精華〗

◉ I'd like to *check-in*, please. 我要登記住宿。

◉ *Do you have a reservation with us*, sir?
　 先生，您有沒有預約？

Dialogue: *C* = **Clerk** 櫃枱職員　　*G* = **Guest** 旅客

C : Good afternoon. Welcome to the Hilton Hotel. May I help you, sir?

C : 午安，歡迎光臨希爾頓飯店。能為您效勞嗎？

G : Yes. I'd like to *check-in*, please.

G : 我要登記住宿。

C : Certainly, sir. May I have your name, please?

C : 好的，請問大名？

G : Yes, it's Robert Zimmerman.

G : 我叫勞勃特‧西摩門。

C : *Do you have a reservation with us*, sir?

C : 先生，您有沒有預約？

G : Yes, for tonight.

G : 有的，預約今晚。

C : Just a moment, please. I'll check our reservation record. ......
Thank you for waiting, sir. Your reservation is for a single room for three nights. Could you *fill out the registration card*, please?

C : 請稍候，我查一下預約記錄。
......

讓您久等了，您預約三個晚上的單人房。請填寫這張登記卡好嗎？

G : Sure...... (*fills out card*)

G : 好的……（填寫卡片）

C : May I *reconfirm your departure date*?

C : 請再確認您哪一天離開好嗎？

G : Yes. I should be leaving on the 5th.

G : 好的，我會在 5 號離開。

C : How would you like to *make payment*?

C : 您要如何付款？

G : By American Express Card.

G : 用全美運通信用卡。

C : *May I take a print of the card*, please? Thank you, sir. Your room is #543 on the 5th Floor. Just a moment please. *A bellman will show you to your room*. I hope you will enjoy your stay.

C : 讓我劃印您的信用卡好嗎？謝謝您，先生。您的房間是五樓 543 號房。請稍候，服務生會帶您過去，希望您住得愉快。

1 Our *check-in time* is 2 o'clock. Would you mind waiting until then?

我們登記住宿的時間是兩點鐘，您介不介意等到那時候？

2 I'm afraid your room is not ready yet. Would you mind waiting, please? *We're very sorry for the inconvenience.*

您的房間恐怕還没準備好。您介不介意稍等一會?抱歉使您不方便。

3 Could you keep your room key until you check out?

請保存您的房間鑰匙直到結完帳好嗎？

** *fill out* "填好"

　registration 〔,rɛdʒɪ'streʃən〕 *n.* 登記

　departure 〔dɪ'partʃə〕 *n.* 離開

　American Express Card 全美運通信用卡

尖峯時間的入宿登記
Check-in at a Busy Time

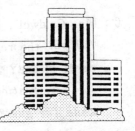

〘 對話精華 〙

◉ I have a reservation *with* you. 我在貴店預訂了房間。

◉ Could you *fill out* the registration card, please？
請填寫住宿登記卡好嗎？

◉ How would you like to *settle your bill*？
您預備如何付款呢？

Dialogue: *C* = **Clerk** 櫃枱職員　　*G* = **Guest** 旅客

C : Good afternoon. Welcome
to the Gloria Hotel. May
I help you？

C：午安，歡迎光臨華泰大飯店。
能為您效勞嗎？

G : Yes. I have a reservation with you.

G：我在貴店預訂了房間。

C : Thank you, sir. ***May I
have your family name***,
please？

C：謝謝您，先生，請問您貴姓？

G : Yes, it's Caldwell.

G：好的，我姓卡得威爾。

C : Mr. Caldwell. Could you *fill out* the registration card, please？ (*Checks the registration record while the guest is filling out the registration card*)

C : 卡得威爾先生，請填寫住宿登記卡好嗎？（趁客人填寫登記卡時，翻查登記記錄）

C : *According to* our records, your reservation is for a twin room for three nights. The room rate will be NT$1,000 per night *excluding a* 10% *tax and a* 10% *service charge*. Will that be all right？

C : 根據我們的記錄，您預約了三個晚上的雙人房。不包括10%的稅金和10%的服務費，房間**費**每晚台幣1,000元。這樣對不對？

G : Yes.

G : 對。

C : *How would you like to settle your bill*？

C : 您預備如何付款呢？

G : By credit card.

G : 用信用卡。

C : May I *take a print* of your card, please？ Thank you, sir. Your room number is 345 on the Third Floor. Have an enjoyable stay.

C : 請讓我劃印您的信用卡好嗎？

謝謝，您的房間是三樓的345號房。祝您住得愉快。

** *family name* 姓　　*according to* 根據；依照
　exclude〔ɪk'sklud〕*v.* 除外　　settle〔'sɛtl〕*v.* 償付
　cardit card 信用卡

旅館的計價方式

目前旅館的計價方式，主要有下列五種。

1. **歐式計價方式** *European Plan*（EP）：
　只計房租，不包括餐飲費用。

2. **美式計價方式** *American Plan*（AP）：
　包括房間費用及三餐餐費在內。

3. **修正美式計價方式** *Modified American Plan*（MP）：
　包括房間費用及二餐餐費（早餐或午餐、晚餐任選）。

4. **歐陸式計價方式** *Continental Plan*（CP）：
　包括房間費用及歐陸式早餐（Continental Breakfast）。

5. **百慕達計價方式** *Bermuda Plan*（BP）：
　包括房間費用及美式早餐（American Breakfast）。

　一般旅行社在訂房時，會在訂房單上註明計價方式，個人預約訂房時，也應該指明。通常旅館的房間費用說明單（Room Tariff），均有標明收費方式。台灣地區各旅館，都以歐式計價方式（EP）計算。

確認難懂的姓名
Confirmation of Difficult Surnames

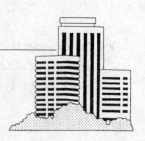

〘 對話精華 〙

◉ *I'm booked for tonight*. 我預約今天晚上。

◉ How do you spell that, please? 請問怎麼拼呢？

Dialogue❶ : *C* = **Clerk** 櫃枱職員　　*G* = **Guest** 旅客

C : Good afternoon, sir. May I help you?

C : 先生，午安，能為您效勞嗎？

G : *I'm booked for tonight*.

G : 我預約今天晚上。

C : May I have your name, please?

C : 請問大名？

G : Yes, it's George Williamson.

G : 我是喬治‧威廉森。

C : *How do you spell that*, please?

C : 請問怎麼拼呢？

G : W.I. double L.I.A.M. S.O.N.

G : W.I.兩個L.I.A.M.S.O. N。

C : *May I have your initials*, please?

C : 請告訴我您名字的第一個字母好嗎？

G : G.E.　　　　　　　　　　G : 是 G .E. 。

C : Mr. Williamson. Just a　　C : 威廉森先生，請稍候。
　　moment, please.

Dialogue❷ :

C : Good afternoon, sir. May　C : 先生，午安，能為您效勞嗎？
　　I help you?

G : Yes, my name is Paul　　G : 我叫保羅‧凡肯。
　　van Kan.

C : *Do you have a reservation*　C : 先生，您向本店預約過嗎？
　　with us, sir?

G : Yes.　　　　　　　　　　G : 預約過。

C : Could you fill out the　　C : 請填寫登記卡好嗎？
　　registration card, please?

　　(after standard reg-　　（ 在標準登記入住手續之後 ）
　　istration procedure)

G : Yes.　　　　　　　　　　G : 是的。

C : Your reservation is for a　　C : 凡肯先生，您預約的是兩個
　　suite room for two per-　　　人過兩夜的套房，對不對？
　　sons for two nights, Mr.
　　van Kan. Is that right?

G : That's right.　　　　　　　G : 是的。

** *suite room* 套房

由公司付帳的入宿登記
On a Company Account

『對話精華』

◉ Your bill will be paid by the Taipei Trade Company.
您的帳單將由台北貿易公司支付。

◉ Please *sign at the Cashier's Counter* when you check out. 結帳時請到會計部簽名。

Dialogue: C = Clerk 櫃枱職員　　G = Guest 旅客

C : Good afternoon. May I help you?

C : 午安，能為您效勞嗎？

G : Yes, my name is James Crimble.

G : 好的，我叫詹姆斯・古林柏。

C : *Do you have a reservation with us*, sir?

C : 您向本店預約過嗎？

G : Yes.

G : 預約過。

C : Thank you, sir. Just a moment, please.

C : 謝謝您，先生，請稍候。

C : Thank you for waiting, sir. Could you *fill out the registration card*, please?

（*after standard registration procedure*）

C : Mr. Crimble. Your reservation is for a twin room for 6 nights and *your bill will be paid by* the Taipei Trade Company. *Could you sign at the Cashier's Counter* when you check out, please?

G : Fine.

C : Your room is #625 on the 6th Floor. A bellman will *show* you *to* your room. Please *enjoy your stay*.

G : Thanks, I will.

C : 先生，讓您久等了，請填寫這張登記卡，好嗎？

（在標準登記手續之後）

C : 古林柏先生，您預約六個晚上的雙人房，帳單由台北貿易公司支付。結帳時請到會計部簽名好嗎？

G : 好的。

C : 您的房間是6樓625號房。服務生會帶您去，請好好休息。

G : 謝謝，我會的。

活用練習

1　Mr. Smith, your reservation is for a single room for 4
nights. Your room charge, ***including tax and service*** will
be paid by the Industry Bristol Ltd. ***Could you settle any
incidental charges yourself***, when you check out, please?

　　史密斯先生，您預約四晚的單人房。您的房錢，包括稅金與服務費
將由必治妥公司支付。結帳時請自行支付雜費好嗎？

　　** ***cashier's counter***　會計部
　　　　include〔ɪnˈklud〕*v.* 包括
　　　incidental charges　雜費

顧客持有預付收據時
With a Hotel Voucher

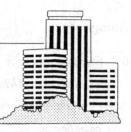

∬ **對話精華** ∬

◉ My travel agent *issued me this hotel voucher*.
　我的旅行社交給我這張預付旅館費用的收據。

◉ I'm afraid this is *only a confirmation note* not a
　voucher. 這張恐怕只是預約確認單而非收據。

Dialogue ❶ : *C* = **Clerk** 櫃枱職員　　*G* = **Guest** 旅客

(*after standard reg-　　　　*（ 在標準登記入住手續之後 ）
istration procedure)

C : *How would you like to*　　　C : 您預備如何付款？
　make payment?

G : *My travel agent issued*　　G : 我的旅行社交給我這張預付
　me this hotel voucher.　　　　旅館費用的收據，我可以使
　Can I use it?　　　　　　　　用嗎？

C : That will be fine. Could　　C : 可以。結帳時請到會計部簽
　you sign at the Cashier's　　　名好嗎？
　Counter when you check
　out, please?

　　** *travel agent* 旅行社　　　**issue** 〔ˈɪʃju〕*v.* 發給
　　hotel voucher 預付旅館費用的收據

Dialogue❷ :

C : Excuse me, sir, but I'm afraid that *this is only a confirmation note not a voucher*.

C : 對不起，這恐怕只是預約確認單而非收據。

G : Really, how's that?

G : 眞的，怎麼會那樣呢？

C : Do you have any other *documents* ?

C : 您還有其他證件嗎？

G : No, this is all I was given.

G : 沒有，這是我拿到的所有東西。

C : I'm very sorry, sir, but could you *settle your bill when you check out*, please?

C : 很抱歉，還是請您結帳時付清帳單好嗎？

活 用 練 習

① Do you have any of these credit cards?
您有沒有這些公司的信用卡？

② *This coupon only covers* the room charges plus the tax and service charges. Could you *settle any incidental charges* when you check out, please?
這張優待券只包括房錢和稅金、服務費，結帳時請付清雜費好嗎？

** document〔ˈdɑkjəmənt〕*n.* 證件　　　　coupon〔ˈkupɑn〕*n.* 優待券

6

確認付款方式
Confirmation of Way of Payment

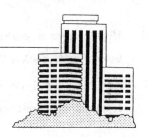

∮ 對話精華 ∮

◉ How would you like to *settle your bill*? 您打算如何付款？

◉ *By credit card.* 用信用卡。

Dialogue: *C* = **Clerk** 櫃枱職員　　*G* = **Guest** 旅客

(*after standard reg-
istration procedure*)　　（在標準入住登記手續之後）

C : *How would you like to
settle your bill*?

C：您打算如何付款？

G : By credit card, but I'd
like to settle my parents'
bill *as well.*

G：用信用卡，我雙親的帳單也
由我結算。

C : Certainly, sir. You would
like to pay the bills of
rooms 876 and 875 to-
gether?

C：好的，您要一併支付876和
875號房的帳單嗎？

G : Yes, please.

G：是的。

C : *May I take a print of your card*, please?

C：請讓我劃印您的信用卡好嗎？

G : Why? Can't I do it when I check out instead?

G：為什麼呢？我不能結帳時再劃印嗎？

C : We ask all our guests to do this *to ensure a smooth and rapid check out at busy times*.

C：我們要求所有客人這麼做，以確保在忙碌時段順利而迅速地結帳。

G : Well, if that's the case .... here you are.

G：好吧，既然是這樣…拿去吧。

C : Thank you, sir. Just a moment, please.

C：謝謝，先生，請稍候。

 活 用 練 習

1 How would you like to *settle your account*? 您打算如付款？

2 *In what form will payment be made*? 您要怎麼付帳？

3 Cash or credit card? 付現金或用信用卡？

4 I'm afraid we don't accept credit cards.
我們恐怕不接受信用卡。

** *as well* "也；同樣地"
   ensure 〔ɪnˈʃʊr〕 v. 確保
   smooth 〔smuð〕 adj. 順利的
   account 〔əˈkaʊnt〕 n. 帳目

7

無預約記錄且旅館客滿時
When Reservation Can't Be Located

〜〜 ∬ **對話精華** ∬ 〜〜

● I'm afraid we have no record of your reservation. *Where was it made*?
我們恐怕沒有你們的預約記錄，您在哪裡預約的？

● It was made about two weeks ago *through our travel agents*. 是大約兩個星期以前透過旅行社代辦的。

Dialogue: *C* = **Clerk** 櫃枱職員　　*G* = **Guest** 旅客

　　　　(*after checking the reservation record*)　　　　（檢查預約記錄之後）

C : Thank you for waiting, sir. I'm afraid we have no record of your reservation. *Where was it made*?

C : 先生，讓您久等了，我們恐怕沒有你們的預約記錄。您在哪裡預約的？

G : That's very strange. It was made about two weeks ago *through our travel agents* at home, Orient Tours, Pasadena, California.

G : 這就怪了。我們是大約兩個星期前在家裡，透過加州巴沙地納的東方旅行社代辦的。

C : Just a moment, please. I'll check our reservation record again. ……
Thank you for waiting, sir. I'm afraid we have no record of any reservation made by Orient Tours *in your name. Do you have a confirmation letter*?

C：請稍等，我再查查預約記錄。……

讓您久等了，我們恐怕沒有東方旅行社以您的名義所做的預約記錄，您有確認函嗎？

G : No, we don't, we only have a copy of our itinerary.

G：沒有，我們只有一張影印的旅程表。

C : May I see it, please?…… I'm afraid this won't be enough.

C：請給我看一下好嗎？…… 這恐怕不夠充份。

G : Well, do you have a room for us?

G：那麼，貴店有沒有我們可住的房間？

C : I'm very sorry sir, but our rooms are *fully booked* for the next week.

C：很抱歉，本店一直到下星期的房間全都額滿了。

G : That's crazy! Where are we going to find a room at this time of day?

G：眞糊塗！這時候叫我們到哪裏去找房間呢？

C : *Shall I find another hotel for you*?

C：我另外替你們找一家旅館好嗎？

G : Yes, please do and make it quick !

G：好的，麻煩你快一點！

C : Certainly sir. I'll *book* you *into* a hotel in this area. Just a moment, please. ……

C：好的，我幫你們預約一家本區的旅館，請稍候。

活用練習

① Where was the reservation *made* ? 是在哪裡預約的？

② Who was the reservation *made by* ? 是誰預約的？

③ Who was the reservation *made through* ?
這預約是透過誰辦理的？

** *travel agent* 旅行社
confirmation letter 確認函
itinerary 〔aɪ'tɪnə,rɛrɪ〕 *n.* 旅程表
crazy 〔'krezɪ〕 *adj.* 糊塗的；瘋狂的

A Room with A View

8 再度光臨而房間費不同時

Room Rate Changes for a Returning Guest

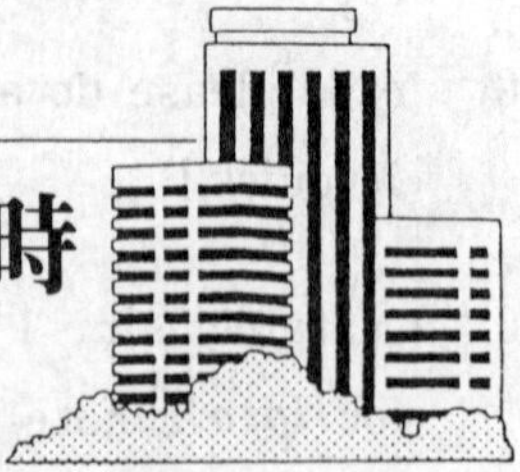

〖對話精華〗

▲ Would you mind having a single room at a lower rate *as the hotel is full*?

因爲旅館客滿，您介不介意住費用較低廉的單人房呢？

▲ When a semi-double is free, please *book* me *into* that.

有空的雙人床位的單人房時，請把我排進去。

Dialogue ❶ : *C* = **Clerk** 櫃枱職員　*G* = **Guest** 旅客

(*when the guest's usual room is not available*)

（當旅客慣常住的房間沒有空房時）

C: I'm afraid your usual semi-double single is not available today. ***We apologize for the inconvenience***, but would you mind having a single room ***at a lower rate*** as the hotel is full?

C：您往常住的雙人床位的單人房，今天恐怕沒有空房。非常抱歉使您不便，因爲旅館客滿，您介不介意住費用較低廉的單人房呢？

G: No, of course not, but when a semi-double is free, please book me into that.

G：當然不介意，但是有空的雙人床位的單人房時，請把我排進去。

C : Certainly, sir. I think one should be available the day after tomorrow. We will *make the change* at that time.

C：好的，先生。我想後天會有一間空出來，我們那時候會替您更換。

Dialogue ❷ :

　　(*when the guest is assigned a lower grade room at the same room rate*)

（當旅客以同等價格分配到較差的房間時）

C : Your reservation is for a single room for three nights, *at a room rate of* NT$1,200 *per night*.

C：您預約每晚房間費1,200元台幣的單人房三個晚上。

G : Why NT$1,200? I stayed here in a twin room the last time at that rate. Why is it a single this time?

G：為什麼要1,200元？我上次住這兒的雙人房也是這個價錢。為什麼這次是單人房呢？

C : *Our standard room rate for a single room is* NT$1,200. I'm afraid there were no single rooms available at that time and *we booked you a twin room at the single room rate*. However, there are single rooms available today. *Will that suit you*?

C：本店標準的單人房錢是台幣1,200元。恐怕是那時候沒有空的單人房，所以我們以單人房的費用為您登記雙人房，然而今天有空的單人房，適合您嗎？

** **semi-double single** 雙人床位的單人房

apologize 〔ə'pɑlə‚dʒaɪz〕 *v*. 道歉

rate 〔ret〕 *n*. 費用

free 〔fri〕 *adj*. (房間等) 空的

assign 〔ə'saɪn〕 *v*. 分配

standard 〔'stændəd〕 *n*. 標準

suit 〔sjut〕 *v*. 適合於；使滿意

⑨ 旅行團的入宿登記
Tour Group Check-in

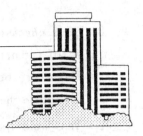

~~~ ∬ 對話精華 ∬ ~~~

◖ Who is the *Tour Leader*, please？請問貴團領隊是誰？

◖ *Is there any change in* the number of your group？
貴團人數有沒有改變？

Dialogue： *TL*= **Tour Leader** 旅行團領隊　　*C* = **Clerk** 職員

C： Good afternoon. *Who is the Tour Leader*, please？

C：午安，請問貴團領隊是誰？

TL： That's me.

TL：我就是。

C： How do you do? My name is Steve of the Front Desk. Welcome to our hotel. *I'd like to reconfirm the schedule for the period of your stay.*

C：您好，我是櫃枱職員史蒂夫，歡迎光臨本店，我想確定一下你們停留期間的時間表。

TL： I see.

TL：哦。

C： Is there any change in the number of your group？

C：貴團人數有沒有改變？

TL： No.

TL：沒有。

C : Your *check-out time* is at 8:00 tomorrow morning. Has there been any change in your schedule?

C : 你們明早八點結帳，貴時間表有任何變動嗎？

TL : Yes. We'd like to change our check-out time to 8:30 a.m.

TL : 有，我們把結帳時間改成早上八點半。

C : 8:30 a.m. Certainly, sir. *We will arrange a morning call at* 7:30 a.m. Will that be fine?

C : 早上八點半，好的。早上七點半我們會安排叫醒電話，這樣好嗎？

TL : That's fine.

TL : 好的。

C : Could you place your bags in front of your room door by 8:00 a.m.? The bellman will *pick* them *up*. Will there be anything else?

C : 請在早上八點以前把行李放在房門口好嗎？服務生會收取，還有什麼事情嗎？

TL : No. That's all.

TL : 沒有了。

C : If there is any change, *could you notify the Front Desk*, please? Please enjoy your stay.

C : 若有任何變動，請通知櫃枱好嗎？祝您在本店住得愉快。

** schedule〔'skɛdʒʊl〕*n.* 時間表

一、團體入住登記手續

1. 接待員依訂房組資料安排房間。

2. 房間安排妥當後，將房間鑰匙置於團體住進專用櫃枱，在此分發鑰匙及宣布注意事項。

3. 向導遊（*Tour Guide*）索取一份正確的團體名單（*Group Rooming List*），迅速整理，分發給各相關部門。

4. 製作團體活動表，包括：叫醒時間（*morning call*）、用餐的種類及時間、餐券（*meal coupon*）、下行李時間（*baggage down*）、遷出時間（*check-out time*），並分送各相關單位。

二、個人旅客入住登記手續

1. 請問客人姓名及是否訂房，立即查看當日訂房單。

2. 由旅客親自填寫旅客登記卡（*Guest Registration*），填寫項目包括姓名、國籍（*Nationality*）、出生年月日（*Date of Birth*）、護照號碼（*Passport Number*）、簽證種類（*Kind of Visa*）及日期（*Date*）、結帳離去時間（*Check-out Date*）、住址（*Home Address*）、簽名（*Signature*）。

3. **問清客人的結帳方式**，如果用信用卡，可先將卡片刷好，離去時簽字即可，以避免結帳時擁擠。

4. 登記完畢後，借旅客護照以查看是否與所填資料相符，然後交與房間鑰匙。提醒客人將貴重物品寄存收銀組保險箱內。

5. 登記手續完成後，利用客房指示器（*Room Indicator*）通知該樓客房服務人員，同時傳叫行李服務員（*Bellman*）提送行李，引導客人至房間。

Instructions to Group Guests

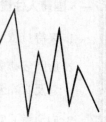

C : Good afternoon. Welcome to the Leofoo Hotel.

1. Your room keys and breakfast **meal vouchers** are in the envelopes on this desk. They are arranged in **alphabetical order**. Please take the one which bears your name.

2. Breakfast will be served from 7 a.m. tomorrow at the Coffee Shop on the First Floor. Could you **hand** your meal voucher **to** the waiter when you arrive there?

3. The Lobby is on the 2nd floor. Please press the L button in the elevator.

4. The door of your room locks automatically. Please **make sure** that you have your room key when you leave the room. You may keep your room key until you check out.

5. **Room-to-room calls** may be made from your room. Please dial 6 first and then the room number.

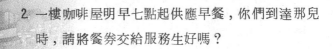

對團體顧客的説明練習

C： 午安，歡迎光臨六福客棧。

1. 你們的房間鑰匙和早餐餐券都在桌上的信封裏，信封是按姓名字母的順序排列的，請拿寫有您名字的那一個。

2. 一樓咖啡屋明早七點起供應早餐，你們到達那兒時，請將餐券交給服務生好嗎？

3. 大廳在二樓，請按電梯中的 L 鈕。

4. 你們房間的門是自動上鎖的，離開房間時請確定您是否帶鑰匙，你們可以保留鑰匙直到結帳。

5. 你們可以從房間直接打電話到別的房間，請先撥 6，然後撥房間號碼。

6. **Outside calls** may be made from your room. Please dial 0 first and then the number.

7. Please read the emergency instructions on your room door. Your nearest emergency exit is also shown.

8. Could you pay any incidental charges at the Front Cashier's Desk when you check out? You may **hand in** your room key at that time.

9. We will deliver your baggage to your room soon. Could you place your bags in front of your room by 7:30 a.m. tomorrow morning? The bellman will collect them.

10. Your **departure time** is at 9:00 a.m. Could you be here by 8:50 a.m. at the latest?

** **envelope** 〔'ɛnvə,lop〕 *n.* 信封；封袋
   alphabetical 〔,ælfə'bɛtɪk]〕 *adj.* 字母的

6. 可以從房間直接撥電話到外面，請先撥 0 再撥電話號碼。

7. 請看門上的緊急出口說明，其上並標示有最近的緊急出口。

8. 結帳時，請到會計部付清雜費，好嗎？屆時可以交回房間鑰匙。

9. 我們會儘快將行李送到你們的房間，請於明晨七點半以前將行李放在門口好嗎？服務生會去收取。

10. 你們早上九點離開，請最遲八點五十分以前來到這裏好嗎？

** **bear**〔bɛr〕*n.* 寫有；印有　　*room-to-room call* 房間直撥電話
emergency instructions 緊急出口說明

遷出時間各旅館可能不盡相同，一般定在當天中午十二時。**逾時遷出**的狀況，在下午六點以前，增收半日租金；越過下午六點則收全日租金。若遇特殊情形，逾時不收租金，須由值班副理簽證。

* 登記房間時，旅客及服務人員皆需了解各種客房的種類以方便登記，以下是幾種客房常見的分類：

(1) 單人房，單人床（ *single room ， single bed* ）

(2) 單人房，雙人床（ *single room ， double bed* ）

(3) 雙人房，雙人床（ *double room ， double bed* ）

(4) 雙人房，單人床二張（ *double room ， twin beds* ）

(5) 三人房（ *triple room* ）

(6) 套房（ *suite* ）

(7) 向內房（ *inside room* ）：無窗或窗子向天井的房間。

(8) 向外房（ *outside room* ）：窗子向街道或公園的房間。

(9) 連接房（ *connecting room* ）：兩相連房間，中間有門。

(10) 鄰接房（ *adjoining room* ）：兩相鄰房間，中間無門。

單（雙）人房有浴室稱為 *single（double）with bath*，簡寫為 SWB（DWB），無浴室為 *single（double）without bath*，簡寫為 SW／OB（DW／OB），只有淋浴設備為 *single（double）with shower*，簡寫為 SW／Shower（DW／Shower）。

Part 6

提供各項資料
Information

1

詢問客房號碼時
Room Number Information

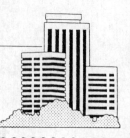

∥ **對話精華** ∥

◉ I'd like to *speak to* Mr. John Crowe.
我要找約翰・克勞先生聽電話。

◉ Mr. Crowe *is staying in* Room #2842.
克勞先生住2842號房。

◉ I'll transfer your call. Could you *hold the line*, please? 我幫您把電話轉過去，請稍等別掛斷電話好嗎？

Dialogue : *C* = Clerk 職員　*G* = Guest 旅客

(on the telephone)　　　　　　　　（電話中）

C : Good morning. This is the Information Desk. May I help you, sir?

C : 詢問台，您早，能爲您效勞嗎？

G : Yes. I'd like to speak to Mr. John Crowe. Could you tell me his room number?

G : 是的，我要找約翰・克勞先生聽電話。你能告訴我他的房間號碼嗎？

C : Certainly, sir. ***How do you spell his last name***, please?

C : 好的，先生，請問他的姓怎麼拼？

G : C. R. O. W. E.

G : C, R, O, W, E。

C : Thank you, sir. Just a
moment, please. ……
Thank you for waiting, sir.
Mr. Crowe is staying in
Room #2842. *Are you*
calling from outside, sir ?

C：謝謝您，先生，請稍候。…

讓您久等了，克勞先生住在
2842號房，先生，這是外
線電話嗎？

G : Yes.

G：是的。

C : *I'll transfer your call.*
Could you hold the line,
please?

C：我幫您把電話轉過去，請稍
等別掛斷電話好嗎？

活 用 練 習

①　I'm afraid *we cannot transfer calls from the house phone*.
Could you dial the number directly, please?
內線電話恐怕無法轉接。請您直撥那個號碼好嗎？

②　*For room-to-room calls*, please dial 6 first and then the
room number.
要從客房打電話到客房，請先撥6再撥房間號碼。

③　The house phones are *around the corner to the right*. Could
you dial the room directly, please?
飯店內線電話在右邊轉角附近。請直撥到客房好嗎？

** *Information Desk* 詢問台
transfer 〔træs'fɚ〕*v*. 轉移
house phone 內線電話
corner 〔'kɔrnɚ〕*n*. 角落

2

所查詢姓名未列在表上
The Name Doesn't Appear on the List

〟 對話精華 〟

◉ I'm afraid his name does not *appear on the list*.
他的 名字恐怕沒登記在名單上。

◉ Mr. Seligman *is booked for today* but he has not checked in yet.
謝里格曼先生是預約今天，但是他尚未辦理住宿登記。

Dialogue : *C* = **Clerk** 職員　*G* = **Guest** 旅客

(check the staying guest list) 　　（檢查住宿旅客一覽表）

C : Thank you for waiting, sir. I'm afraid his name does not ***appear*** on the list. ***When is he due to arrive***?

C : 讓您久等了，他的名字恐怕沒登記在名單上，他預定何時抵達。

G : Today.

G : 今天。

C : I see, sir. I'll check our reservation list. Could you hold the line, please? ……
Thank you for waiting. Mr. Seligman is ***booked for*** today but he has not ***checked in*** yet.

C : 先生，我查一下預約表，請別掛斷好嗎？……

讓您久等了，謝里格曼先生是預約今天，但是他尚未辦理住宿登記。

G：O.K. I'll call again later.　　　　G：好的，我待會兒再打來。

活 用 練 習

① I'm afraid he has already checked out. 他恐怕已經退宿了。

② I'm afraid we do not know at what time he left the hotel.
我們恐怕不知道他什麼時候離開旅館的。

③ I'm afraid *he left no forwarding address*.
他恐怕並未留下下一站的地址。

④ I'm afraid he has cancelled his reservation.
他恐怕已經取消預約了。

⑤ I'm afraid he is not *occupying* that room. 他恐怕不住那間房。

⑥ I'm afraid *there's no guest with that name*. We have a guest
with a similar name. Would that be him? 恐怕沒有叫那個名字
的客人。我們有一位名字相近的客人，會不會是他？

⑦ Who would you like *to contact* (*to call, to leave a message
for*)? 您想聯絡（打電話給，留話給）誰？

＊＊ **appear**〔ə'pɪr〕*v.* 出現　　**due**〔dju〕*adj.* 應到的；預期的
forwarding address 下一站預定停留的地址，以供轉寄信件等
occupy〔'ɑkjə,paɪ〕*v.* 居住
similar〔'sɪmələ〕*adj.* 相似的
leave a message "留言"

3
留言給住宿旅客
Message for a Staying Guest

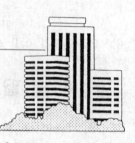

~ 〖 對話精華 〗 ~

◉ Could you *take a message* for him, please?
請留言給他好嗎?

◉ *May I know who is calling*, please? 請問您哪裏找?

◉ I will repeat your message. 我覆述一次您的留言。

Dialogue ❶ : *C* = **Clerk** 職員   *JE* = **James Ellens** 詹姆士・艾倫斯
G = **Gulbenkian** 古爾班肯

C : This is the Information Desk. May I help you?

G : 詢問台,能為您效勞嗎?

JE : I tried to contact Mr. Gulbenkian in Room 834 but he was out. Could you *take a message* for him, please?

JE : 我試圖聯絡834號房的古爾班肯先生,但是他一直不在。請留言給他好嗎?

C : Certainly, sir. For Mr. Gulbenkian in Room 834. *May I know who is calling*, please?

C : 好的,留言給834號房的古爾班肯先生,請問您哪裏找?

JE : Yes. My name is James Ellens.

JE : 我叫詹姆士・艾倫斯。

C : Mr. Ellens. *Go ahead, please.*

C : 艾倫斯先生，請說。

JE : Could you ask him to *call me back* as soon as he arrives at the hotel ?

JE : 請他到達旅館後立刻回電話給我好嗎？

C : Certainly, sir. May I have your number, please ?

C : 好的，您的電話是幾號？

JE : Yes, it's Taipei 234 – 4273.

JE : 台北234 – 4273。

C : Taipei 234 – 4273 ?

C : 是台北234 – 4273 嗎？

JE : That's right.

JE : 是的。

C : *Is that the* (*complete*) *message* ?

C : 這就是（全部的）留言嗎？

JE : Yes, that's all.

JE : 是的，就這樣。

C : Certainly, sir. *I will repeat your message.* The message is for Mr. Gulben-kian in Room #834 from Mr. James Ellens. please *call* him *back* at 234 – 4273 when you arrive at the hotel. Is that *correct* ?

C : 好的，我覆述一次您的留言。詹姆士‧艾倫斯先生留言給834號房的古爾班肯先生。請到達旅館時回電234 – 4273給他，對不對？

JE : That's right.

JE : 對的。

C : Thank you very much. My name is Helen. If you have any *further enquiries, please don't hesitate to contact me.*

C : 謝謝您，我叫海倫，如果您想詢問任何更進一步的資料，請別客氣儘量與我聯絡。

Dialogue ❷ :

C : Information Desk. May I help you?

C : 詢問台，能爲您效勞嗎？

G : Yes, my name is Gulbenkian in Room #834. *My message lamp is on*. Is there a message for me?

G : 是的，我是834號房的古爾班肯，我的留言灯亮著，有給我的留言嗎？

C : Yes. *There is a message for you from* Mr. James Ellens.

C : 是的，有詹姆士・艾倫斯先生給您的留言。

G : Could you read it for me, please?

G : 請唸給我聽好嗎？

C : Mr. Ellens called at 3:15 p. m. *He asked you to call him back* as soon as you returned. His number is 234-4273.

C : 艾倫斯先生下午3點15分打電話來，他要您回來後立卽回電給他。他的電話是234-4273。

G : Fine. Thanks very much.

G : 好的，謝謝。

C : You're welcome, sir.

C : 不客氣，先生。

活 用 練 習

① May I have the message, please?
請告訴我您的留言好嗎？

② *Is he a hotel guest*? 他是旅館的客人嗎？

③ I'm afraid we can only *take messages for* staying guests, and those *with future reservations*.

我們恐怕只能爲住店的客人以及那些已經預約的客人傳話。

④ I'm afraid that Mr. Williamson is not a guest at the hotel, and we have no reservation *in his name*.

威廉森先生恐怕不是旅館的客人，我們也沒有以他的名字訂的預約。

⑤ I'm afraid we can only *take* simple messages.

我們恐怕只能受理簡單的留言。

⑥ Could you call again later, please? 請稍候再打過來好嗎？

⑦ Mr. Lin *is due to check out* today, but we're not sure at what time he is leaving. If he has already checked out, *we will not be able to give him a message*. What would you like us to do? 林先生預計今天結帳，但我們不確定他會什麼時候離開。 如果他已經結了帳，我們就無法傳話給他，您希望我們怎麼做呢？

⑧ Mr. Smith left a message for you *while you were out*.

您不在的時候史密斯先生留話給您。

⑨ Mr. Smith will *pick you up at the hotel* at 6:00 p.m.

史密斯先生下午六點會到旅館來接您。

** *take a message* "留言；傳話" *who is calling* "是誰打（電話）來的" *call back* "回電話"　complete〔kəm'plit〕*adj.* 全部的 repeat〔rɪ'pit〕*v.* 覆述　correct〔kə'rɛkt〕*adj.* 正確的 enquiry〔ɪn'kwaɪrɪ〕*n.* 詢問　hesitate〔'hɛzə,tet〕*v.* 猶豫；言語支吾 lamp〔læmp〕*n.* 燈　*staying guest* 住宿旅館的客人 *guest with future reservation* 已經預約，即將來住宿的客人 simple〔'sɪmpḷ〕*adj.* 簡單的

4 替客人傳話
Guest Location

~~~ 〖 對話精華 〗 ~~~

◉ We will *inform* him when he comes.
他來時我們會轉告他。

◉ He *asked us to tell you* to meet him in the Coffee
Shop. 他要我們告訴您去咖啡廳見他。

Dialogue ❶： *C* = **Clerk** 職員　　*H* = **Mr. Hahn** 哈恩先生
　　　　　　　 D = **Mr. Dacanay** 達克奈先生

C： Good morning, sir. May
I help you?

C：早安，能爲您效勞嗎？

H： Yes. I have a very impor-
tant *client* coming between
9 and 9:30 a.m. but I won't
be in my room. When he
comes, could you tell him
that *I'll be in the Coffee
Shop having breakfast* ?

H：九點到九點半之間，我有一
位很重要的客戶要來，但是
我不會在房間裏。他來時，
請告訴他我在咖啡廳吃早點。

C： Are you a hotel guest?

C：您是旅館的客人嗎？

H： Yes. I'm staying in Room
577.

H：是的，我住 577 號房。

C : May I have your client's
name, please?

C：請問貴客戶的大名？

H : Yes, it's Dacanay of B.T.
Engineering.

H：他是B.T. 工程公司的達克奈
先生。

C : Mr. Dacanay. Thank you,
sir. *We will inform him.*
when he comes. Until what
time will you be in the
Coffee Shop, sir?

C：達克奈先生。謝謝您，他來
時我們會轉告他。先生，您
會在咖啡廳待到幾點？

H : Until 10:00 a.m.

H：待到上午十點。

C : I see, sir.

C：我知道了。

Dialogue❷ :

D : I'd like to meet Mr. Hahn
in Room #577, but he
seems to be out. Do you
know when he will be back?

D：我要見577 號房的哈恩先生,
可是他好像不在，你知道他
幾時回來嗎？

C : May I have your name,
please?

C：請問您貴姓？

D : Yes, it's Dacanay of B.T.
Engineering.

D：是的，我是B.T. 工程公司
的達克奈。

C : Just a moment, please. ⋯
⋯

C：請等一下。⋯⋯

Mr. Hahn will be in the Coffee Shop until 10:00 a.m. *He asked us to tell you to meet him there*.

哈恩先生早上十點以前在咖啡廳。他要我們告訴您去那裏見他。

D : Thank you.

D：謝謝。

C : You're welcome, sir.

C：不客氣，先生。

** **client** 〔'klaɪənt〕 *n*. 客戶
   engineering 〔,ɛndʒə'nɪrɪŋ〕 *n*. 工程

5 介紹臨近場所
For Nearby Locations

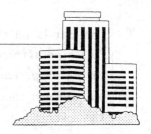

〖 **對話精華** 〗

◬ Excuse me, where is the telephone?
　對不起，請問電話在哪裏？

◬ It's over there *at the back of the elevator hall*.
　在那裏，電梯間的後面。

Dialogue ❶ : 　*G* = **Guest** 旅客　*C* = **Clerk** 職員

G : Excuse me, where is the
　　telephone?

G：對不起，請問電話在哪裏？

C : The *public phone*, ma'am?

C：女士，公用電話嗎？

G : Yes.

G：是的。

C : It's over there *at the back
　of the elevator hall*.

C：在那裏，電梯間的後面。

G : Thanks a lot.

G：謝謝。

C : You're welcome, ma'am.

C：不客氣，女士。

Dialogue ❷ :

G : Could you please tell me
　　how to get to the Bar?

G：請告訴我如何到酒吧好嗎？

C : The Bar is on this floor.
Please *go straight along the*
the hallway, turn right at
the end and the Bar is on
the left.

C：酒吧在這一樓，請沿著走廊
　直走，到盡頭右轉，酒吧就
　在左手邊。

G : Thank you.

G：謝謝。

活 用 練 習

① The cloakroom is over there. 寄物處就在那兒。

② The elevators are *straight ahead on the left.*
電梯在正前方左手邊。

③ The restroom is *at the end of* the hallway *to the right.*
洗手間在走廊盡頭右手邊。

④ The pearl shop is *along the hall* next to the chinaware shop.
沿著走廊走，陶瓷店隔壁就是珠寶店。

⑤ The Airline Counter is *in front of* the flower shop
(*florist's*). 航空公司櫃枱在花店的前面。

⑥ The stairway is *around the corner* over there.
樓梯在那邊的轉角附近。

** straight〔stret〕*adv*. 直地　　hallway〔'hɔl,we〕*n*. 走廊
restroom〔'rɛst,rum〕*n*. 洗手間　　*pearl shop* 珠寶店
chinaware shop 陶瓷店　　stairway〔'stɛr,we〕*n*. 樓梯
complicated〔'kɑmplə,ketɪd〕*adj*. 複雜的

6

介紹較遠的場所
For Faraway Locations

〔 對話精華 〕

◑ Excuse me, where's the Coffee Shop?
對不起，請問咖啡廳在哪裏？

◑ *Go up these stairs* and the Coffee Shop is *to the left.* 走上樓，咖啡廳就在左邊。

Dialogue : *G* = **Guest** 旅客　*C* = **Clerk** 職員

G : Excuse me, where's the Coffee Shop?

G : 對不起，請問咖啡廳在哪裏？

C : The Coffee Shop is on the first floor of the New Wing. *Take the hallway* to the left *past* the Front Desk to the stairs. Go down the stairs and *continue along* to the next set of stairs. *Go up* these stairs and the Coffee Shop is to the left.

C : 咖啡廳在新館的一樓，沿這條走廊左轉，通過櫃枱到樓梯口。走下樓，繼續往前走，到達另一個樓梯口，走上樓，咖啡廳就在左邊。

G : Thank you.

G : 謝謝你。

** **wing** 〔wɪŋ〕 *n.* （建築物等的）邊側突出的部分；廂房
continue 〔kən'tɪnju〕 *v.* 繼續

7
指示客人如何到旅館
Giving Directions to the Hotel

~ ∥對話精華∥ ~

⬥ Could you tell me how to *get to* your hotel?
請告訴我如何到你們的旅館好嗎?

⬥ *Take the small street* beside McDonald's *to the end.*
The hotel is *straight ahead.*
從麥當勞旁邊的小路直走到底,旅館就在正前方。

Dialogue : *C* = **Clerk** 職員　*G* = **Guest** 旅客

C : Information Desk. May I help you?

C : 詢問台,能為您效勞嗎?

G : Yes. Could you tell me how to *get to* your hotel?

G : 請告訴我如何到你們的旅館好嗎?

C : *Where will you be coming from*, sir?

C : 您要從哪裏來?

G : From Taoyuan.

G : 從桃園。

C : I see, sir. Take the airport bus 30 minutes to the Taipei Station. *Leave by the Chung Hsiao East Road Exit.* You will see a McDonald's *across*

C : 知道了,先生。搭機場巴士,三十分鐘就到台北車站。從忠孝東路出口處出來,您會看到街對面右手邊有一間麥當勞。從麥當勞旁邊的小路

the street to the right.
Take the small street be-
side McDonalds to the end.
The hotel is straight ahead.

直走到底，旅館就在正前方。

G： How far is it from the
Station?

G：距離車站有多遠？

C： *It takes about five minutes
on foot.*

C：走路約五分鐘。

G： Thanks a lot.

G：謝謝。

C： You're welcome, sir. We look
forward to seeing you.

C：不客氣，先生。我們期待見
到您。

活 用 練 習

[1] It is on the left out of the station forecourt.
走出車站前廣場就在左手邊。

[2] It's about 3 minutes *on foot* from the station. Turn left *out
of the station. Follow the road,* and it's on the left.
從車站走路約三分鐘。走出車站左轉，沿著那條路走，就在路的左
邊。

[3] Go straight until the road forks. *Take the left fork.*
向前直走到分叉路口，走左邊的那條叉路。

** **forecourt** 〔'for‚kort〕 *n.* （建築物的）前庭；廣場
fork 〔fɔrk〕 *n.* 分叉（處）

指示客人如何到目的地
Giving Directions to the Destination

〖 對話精華 〗

◉ *What's the best way*? 最近的路怎麼走？

◉ Take No. 37 bus from here *three stops to the Taipei Station*. 從這裏搭三十七路公車，坐三站到台北車站。

Dialogue ❶ : *G* = Guest 旅客   *C* = Clerk 職員

G : I want to get to Tansui. What's the best way?

G : 我要去淡水，最近的路怎麼走？

C : Tansui is fifty minutes from the Taipei Station by train. *Take No. 37 bus from here three stops to the Taipei Station*. Change to the Tansui Line and go five stops to Tansui.

C : 從台北車站搭火車到淡水要五十分鐘，從這裏搭三十七路公車，坐三站到台北車站，再換淡水線火車，坐五站就到淡水了。

G : I see. Thanks very much.

G : 我懂了，非常謝謝。

Dialogue ❷ :

G : How do I *get to* the Tainan Station, please?

G : 請問我要怎麼去台南火車站?

C : The Tainan Station is about eight minutes *on foot* from here. Please leave the hotel by the Main Exit over there, turn right, and *take the first left after the inter-section*. The Tainan Station is at the end of the street on the right.

C : 台南火車站從這裏走過去約八分鐘，請從那裏的旅館正門出去，右轉，過了十字路口以後第一次左轉，台南火車站就在街底右手邊。

活 用 練 習

① Shall I *draw you a map*? 要我畫一張地圖給您嗎？

② Shall I *write directions for the taxi driver*? 要我寫下方位給計程車司機嗎？

③ I think it would be better to take a taxi, sir. 先生，我想搭計程車比較好。

④ Do you know the address, sir? 先生，您知道地址嗎？

⑤ Most taxi drivers do not speak English. 大部份的計程車司機不講英文。

⑥ It is helpful if you *have your destination written in Chinese*. 如果用中文寫下您要去的地方，將會很便利。

⑦ We can tell the taxi driver your destination. 我們可以告訴計程車司機您的目的地。

⑧ *Where would you like to go*? 您想去哪裏?

⑨ The Bell Captain can give you a map of Taipei.
領班可以給您一張台北地圖。

⑩ When you return to the hotel, please *show this hotel card
to the taxi driver*.
當您回旅館的時候,請給計程車司機看這張旅館的名片。

** intersection〔ˌɪntɚˈsɛkʃən〕*n.* 十字路口;交叉點
destination〔ˌdɛstəˈneʃən〕*n.* 目的地

9

提供逛街觀光資料
Information for Shopping & Sightseeing

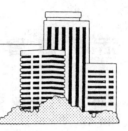

〖 對話精華 〗

◐ I'd like to buy a stereo set. *Where's the best place to go*? 我想買一套音響，最好去什麼地方？

◓ There are many *electrical discount shops* there. 那兒有許多廉價的電器商店。

Dialogue : *C* = **Clerk** 職員　*G* = **Guest** 旅客

C : Good morning, sir. May I help you?

C：先生，早安，能爲您效勞嗎？

G : I'd like to buy *a stereo set*. Where's the best place to go?

G：我想買一套音響，最好去什麼地方？

C : *The best place is* Chung Hua Road. There are many *electrical discount shops* there. It's about 20 minutes by taxi from here.

C：最好是去中華路，那兒有許多廉價的電器商店，從這兒搭計程車約二十分鐘。

G : That sounds fine. Thanks a lot.

G：聽起來挺不錯的。謝謝。

C : You're welcome, sir.

C：不客氣，先生。

活 用 練 習

1 *There are many tours to Tainan offered by* the travel agent in the hotel.
　旅館裏的旅行社提供各種往台南的旅行團。

2 Here is a *pamphlet* explaining the tours offered.
　這本手册介紹各種提供的旅行團。

3 Could you ask at the travel agents over there, please? *They will give you further details.*
　請詢問那兒的旅行社好嗎？他們會提供您更詳細的資料。

4 I'm afraid the …… *Museum* is closed on Mondays.
　該博物館星期一恐怕不開放。

**　stereo 〔'stɛrɪo〕 *n.* 立體音響
　　discount 〔'dɪskaʊnt〕 *n.* 折扣
　　offer 〔'ɔfɚ〕 *v.* 提供
　　pamphlet 〔'pæmflɪt〕 *n.* 小册子
　　museum 〔mju'ziəm〕 *n.* 博物館

10

親手遞交包裹
Delivery of Packages by Hand

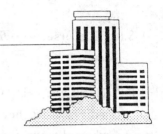

〖**對話精華**〗

◭ I'd like this package to *be delivered to* Mrs. Dickinson in Room #543.

我想把這個包裹交給543號房的狄金生太太。

◭ Could you *fill out this form*, please?

請填寫這張表格好嗎?

Dialogue : *C* = **Clerk** 職員　*S* = **Mr. Smith** 史密斯先生
　　　　　　　D = **Mrs. Dickinson** 狄金生太太

C : Good afternoon, sir. May I help you?

C : 先生,午安,能為您效勞嗎?

S : *I'd like this package to be delivered to* Mrs. Dickinson in Room #543.

S : 我想把這個包裹交給543號房的狄金生太太。

C : Certainly, sir. Is there anything valuable or breakable in the package?

C : 好的,先生,包裹裏有沒有貴重或易碎物品?

S : No, there isn't.

S : 不,沒有。

C : I see, sir. Could you *fill out* this form, please?

C : 我知道了,先生,請填寫這張表格好嗎?

S : Of course. ……*Here you are.*

S：好的，……填好了。

C : Thank you, sir. We will deliver it to her room when when she arrives.

C：謝謝您，先生，她抵達時我們會送到她房裏。

C : *Front Desk speaking.* May I help you?

C：櫃枱，能爲您效勞嗎？

D : This is Mrs. Dickinson in Room #543. My *message lamp is on.* Is there something for me?

D：我是543號房的狄金生太太，我的留言灯亮著，有什麼要給我嗎？

C : Yes, ma'am. There is a package for you from Mr. Smith. Shall we *deliver* it *to* your room?

C：是的，女士。史密斯先生有一個包裹要交給您，要我們送到您的房間去嗎？

D : *Please do.*

D：麻煩你了。

C : Certainly, ma'am. We will deliver it immediately.

C：好的，我們馬上將它送過去。

活 用 練 習

1 Could you *leave* any valuables *with* the Front Cashier,
please?

請把貴重物品寄放在出納處好嗎？

2 Mr. Wilson is checking out today. We are not sure whether
he will go back to his room. If we cannot deliver this,
could you collect it later, please?

威爾遜先生今天要結帳，我們不確定他是否會回房間。如果我們無
法轉交這個，請您稍後來取回好嗎？

** **message** 〔'mɛsɪdʒ〕 *n*. 傳言

immediately 〔ɪ'midɪɪtlɪ〕 *adv*. 立刻

valuable 〔'væljʊəbḷ〕 *n*. (通常作複數) 貴重物品

cashier 〔kæ'ʃɪr〕 *n*. 出納員

11

代客人轉交信件
Forwarding Letters

〖 對話精華 〗

◉ Could you *hand* it *to* him, please？請把這個交給他好嗎？

◉ We will *keep* it *for* him. 我們會為他保留此物。

◉ *May I see some identification*, please？
   請讓我看您的證件好嗎？

Dialogue : *C* = **Clerk** 職員　*R* = **Mr. Rogers** 羅傑茲先生
　　　　　S = **Mr. Sanger** 桑格先生

C : Good afternoon. May I
　　help you, sir？

C：午安，能為您效勞嗎？

R : This is Mr. Rogers in
　　Room 1243. *Mr. Sanger will*
　　come for this while I am
　　out. Could you *hand* it *to*
　　him, please？

R：我是 1243 號房的羅傑茲，在
　　我退宿之後，桑格先生會來
　　拿這個，請你交給他好嗎？

C : Certainly, sir. When will
　　you be checking out？

C：好的，先生，您什麼時候結
　　帳退宿？

R : Tomorrow morning.

R：明天早上。

C : I see, sir. Could you *fill*
　　out this form, please？

C：我知道了，先生，請填寫這
　　張表格好嗎？

R : Sure.······Here you are.

C : Thank you. *We will keep it for him.*

R：當然好。······填好了。

C：謝謝。我們會爲他保留此物。

ⓒ　　　　ⓒ　　　　　　ⓒ

S : My name is Sanger. *I'm expecting a letter from* Mr. Rogers. Do you have anything for me?

C : When did Mr. Rogers *leave* it for you?

S : Yesterday, I think.

C : Just a moment, please. I'll check for you. ······
Thank you for waiting. We have a letter for Mr. Sanger. *May I see some identification*, please?

S : Sure. Here's my *driver's licence*. Is that all right?

C : Thank you, sir. Here you are. Could you *sign* here, please?

S : Thanks.

S：我姓桑格，來拿羅傑兹先生寫的信，你們有沒有什麼要交給我？

C：羅傑兹先生什麼時候留信給您的？

S：我想是昨天。

C：請稍候，我幫您查查看。······

讓您久等了，這裏有一封給桑格先生的信，請讓我看看您的證件好嗎？

S：當然好，這是我的駕照，可以嗎？

C：先生，謝謝。這就是，請在這兒簽名好嗎？

S：謝謝。

C : You're welcome, sir. *Have
   a nice day*.

C：不客氣，先生，祝您今天愉
快。

活 用 練 習

1 When are they expecting to pick it up, sir?
   他們預定什麼時候來拿？

2 Have you *contacted* them about the package, sir?
   先生，您和他們聯絡過包裹的事嗎？

3 If they don't come to collect it, may we *dispose of* it
   after one week?
   如果他們沒有來拿，我們可以在一星期以後廢棄嗎？

4 Do you know *what kind of package* it is?
   您知道那是什麼樣的包裹嗎？

** *fill out* " 填好 "　　**expect**〔ɪk'spɛkt〕*v*. 期待；預期
   identification〔aɪ,dɛntəfə'keʃən〕*n*. 證件
   licence〔'laɪsn̩s〕*n*. 執照
   sign〔saɪn〕*v*. 簽名　　**contact**〔'kɑntækt〕*v*. 聯繫
   dispose of " 除去；廢棄 "

12 遞交・寄送郵件
Delivering & Sending Mail

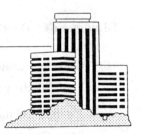

∥對話精華∥

◉ A telex has just arrived for you.
一份給您的交換電報剛剛送到。

◉ I'll come down and *pick it up myself*. 我自己下去拿。

◉ Would you like to send it *by air mail or surface mail*?
您要用航空或海運郵寄？

Dialogue ❶ : *C* = Clerk 職員　*G₁* = a Male Guest 男客人

C : This is the Front Desk. May I speak to Mr. Sachs, please?

C : 這兒是櫃枱，請薩克斯先生接電話好嗎？

G₁ : Speaking.

G₁ : 我就是。

C : A *telex* has just arrived for you. Shall we *deliver* it *to* your room?

C : 一份給您的交換電報剛剛送到，要我們送到您房裏嗎？

G₁ : That's O.K. Could you leave it in my mailbox and *I'll come down and pick it up myself*?

G₁ : 沒關係，把它放在我的信箱，我自己下去拿好嗎？

Dialogue ❷ : *C* = Clerk 職員 *G₂* = a **Female Guest** 女客人

C : Good morning, ma'am. May I help you?

C : 女士，早，能爲您效勞嗎？

G₂ : I'd like to mail this package. Can I send it from here?

G₂ : 我要寄這個小包，可以從這裏郵寄嗎？

C : Certainly, ma'am. Would you like to *send it by air mail or surface mail*?

C : 當然可以。您要用航空或海運郵寄？

G₂ : By air mail, please.

G₂ : 請用航空郵寄。

C : I'll weigh it for you. ⋯⋯ It weighs 2 kilos, and will cost NT$ 800.

C : 我幫您秤秤看。⋯⋯ 重兩公斤，郵費台幣八佰元。

G₂ : *That's expensive!* Could you *charge* it *to* my room bill then?

G₂ : 好貴！請記在我的客房帳單上好嗎？

C : Certainly, ma'am.

C : 好的，女士。

活 用 練 習

1. I'm afraid that *registered mail* can only be sent at the Post Office. 掛號郵件恐怕只能從郵局寄出。

2. It should take about one week to arrive by air mail.
   航空郵件約需一個星期才會到。

3. I'm afraid we cannot *charge* it *to* your room bill. Could you *pay in cash*, please?
   我們恐怕不能記在您的客房帳單上，請付現金好嗎？

4. I'm afraid that this kind of *fastener* is not allowed as it *damages* other items in the post.
   因爲這種釦子會損傷別的郵件，恐怕不允許使用。

** **telex** 〔ˈtɛlɛks〕 *n.* 商務交換電報

　　surface mail 非航空的平常郵件；水陸郵件

　　weigh 〔we〕 *v.* 稱…的重量

　　expensive 〔ɪkˈspɛnsɪv〕 *adj.* 昂貴的

　　charge 〔tʃɑrdʒ〕 *v.* 記帳

　　registered mail 掛號郵件

　　fastener 〔ˈfæsn̩ɚ〕 *n.* 使牢繫之物（指附有金屬釦的信封）

　　damage 〔ˈdæmɪdʒ〕 *v.* 損傷

13

廣播呼叫客人
Paging

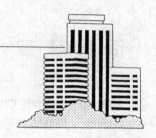

~~~
【 對話精華 】
~~~

⊙ Could you *page* him for me, please?
請幫我廣播叫他好嗎?

◐ Could you *contact* the Front Information Desk,
please? 請與櫃枱詢問處聯絡好嗎?

◑ I heard *my name called over the P.A. System.*
我聽到廣播找我。

Dialogue: *C* = **Clerk** 職員 *T* = **Mr. Thomas** 湯瑪士先生
B = **Mr. Becker** 貝克先生

C: Good afternoon, sir. May
I help you?

C:午安,先生,能爲您效勞嗎?

T: I arranged to meet a friend
here but he hasn't *turned up.*
Could you page him *for me*,
please?

T:我安排在這兒會見一位朋友,
但是他還沒出現,請幫我廣
播叫他好嗎?

C: Certainly, sir. Could you
write down your name and
that of your friend, please?

C:好的,請寫下您以及貴朋友
的大名好嗎?

T: I see. ⋯⋯ Here you are.

T:哦,⋯⋯寫好了。

C : Just a moment, please.……
Paging Mr. Becker, paging
Mr. Becker. Could you
contact the Front Infor-
mation Desk, please?
Thank you.

C：請稍等。……
來賓貝克先生，來賓貝克先
生，請與櫃枱詢問處聯絡好
嗎？謝謝。

B : I heard my name called
over the P.A. System. It's
Becker. What's the problem?

B：我聽到廣播找我，我是貝克，
有什麼事嗎？

C : Mr. Thomas is *waiting for*
you at the Front Desk.
Could you come here, please?

C：湯瑪士先生在櫃枱等您，請
到這兒來好嗎？

B : I see, thanks. Tell him I'll
be there *right away*.

B：我知道了，謝謝。告訴他我
馬上過去。

C : Certainly, sir.

C：好的，先生。

** *turn up* " 出現；來臨 "
page〔pedʒ〕*v.*〔美〕（侍者）喊名找（某人）；（在旅館等）叫侍者去喊人
P.A. System = *Public Address System* 擴音系統（包括麥克風和揚聲喇叭等）

14 領取鑰匙時
Picking up Room Key

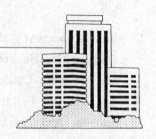

⌇ 『對話精華』⌇

⚫ I'm *in* Room #754. May I have my key, please?
我住754號房。請給我房間鑰匙好嗎?

⚫ Your key, sir, and there is some *registered mail for you.* 先生,您的鑰匙,還有一些您的掛號郵件。

Dialogue: *G* = **Guest** 旅客 *C* = **Clerk** 職員

G: My name is Bush and I'm *in* Room #754. ***May I have my key***, please?

G: 我叫布希,住754號房。請給我房間鑰匙好嗎?

C: Excuse me, sir, but may I see your ***Room Identification Slip***, please?

C: 先生,對不起,請讓我看看您的房間識別證好嗎?

G: Sure. Here it is.

G: 好的,在這兒。

C: Thank you, sir. Could you sign here for receipt of your key, please?

C: 謝謝,請在這裏簽名以領取鑰匙好嗎?

G: Uh-huh.

G: 嗯。

C : Thank you. Your key, sir, and there is some ***registered mail*** for you. Could you sign for that, too?

C：謝謝，先生，您的鑰匙，還有一些您的掛號信，也請一併簽名好嗎？

G : Yes, of course.

G：當然好。

C : Thank you, sir. Have a good night.

C：謝謝您，晚安。

** ***Room Identification Slip*** 房間識別證
　　receipt〔rɪˊsit〕*n.* 領取
　　register〔ˊrɛdʒɪstɚ〕*v.* 掛號

15 因整修而要求客人換房間
Room Change Due to Repairs

〖對話精華〗

◑ I'll get him for you. 我幫你叫他。

◑ We would like to *request you to change your room.*
我們想請您換房間。

◑ I suppose we *have no choice.* 我想我們別無選擇。

Dialogue： *C* = **Clerk** 職員　　*B* = **Mr. Black** 布雷克先生
　　　　　　G = **Mr. Gordon** 戈登先生

C : Good morning. May I speak to Mr. Gordon, please?

C：早，請戈登先生聽電話好嗎?

B : Hold the line, please. *I'll get him for you.*

B：請別掛斷，我幫你叫他。

G : Hello, Gordon speaking.

G：喂，我是戈登。

C : Good morning, Mr. Gordon. This is the Front Desk. I'm afraid that the air conditioning in your room needs repair. We would like to *request you to change your room.* We are very sorry for the *inconvenience.*

C：早，戈登先生，這裏是櫃枱，您房間的空調設備恐怕需要修理了。我們想請您換房間。抱歉為您帶來不便。

G : O.K. Well, I suppose we *have no choice*. What do you want us to do?

G：好的，我想我們別無選擇，你要我們做什麼呢？

C : What time is the most convenient for you to change rooms, sir?

C：先生，你們什麼時間換房間最方便呢？

G : We're going out in about 15 minutes.

G：我們十五分鐘左右就要出去了。

C : What time will you be back?

C：什麼時候回來呢？

G : Oh, *around* three or four o'clock, I suppose.

G：嗯，我想三、四點左右吧。

C : We could move your luggage while you are out, but *could you take any valuables with you*? You may pick up your new room key #883 from the Front Desk when you return.

C：我們可以在你們外出時搬移行李，但是，你們可不可以把貴重物品帶在身上？等回來時就可以在櫃枱領取新的883號房鑰匙。

G : That sounds like the best way. What shall I *do with* the old one?

G：這似乎是最好的方法。原有的鑰匙怎麼處理？

C : Could you *leave* it *at* the Front Desk when you go out, please?

C：請您外出時交給櫃枱好嗎？

G : O.K. I'll do that.

C : Thank you very much indeed, sir. We are very sorry for the inconvenience. *Hope you have a nice day.*

G : Thanks, we will.

G：好的，就這麼辦。

C：先生，眞地非常謝謝您，很抱歉使您不方便。祝您一天愉快。

G：謝謝，會的。

** *air conditioning* 空氣調節設備
request 〔rɪˈkwɛst〕v. 請求
inconvenience 〔ˌɪnkənˈvinjəns〕n. 不便
suppose 〔səˈpoz〕v. 想像；以爲
choice 〔tʃɔɪs〕n. 選擇
do with "處理"

16

想多住幾天卻沒有空房時
Wishing to Extend One's Stay but No Room Available

〖 **對話精華** 〗

◐ *By how many nights* do you wish to *extend*?
　您希望延長幾晚？
　(*How much longer* would you like to stay?)
　您想多住幾天？

◑ I'd like to extend my stay *by two days*.
　我想多住兩天。

Dialogue： *C* = **Clerk** 職員　　*G* = **Guest** 旅客

C : Good afternoon, sir. May I help you?

C：先生，午安，能為您效勞嗎？

G : Yes. I've been a guest in this hotel for the past week and I'm *due to* check out tomorrow, but *I'd like to extend my stay by two or three days.*

G：我在貴店已經住了一個星期，應該明天結帳，但是我想多住兩三天。

C : I see, sir. May I have your name and room number, please?

C：我了解了，先生。請問您的貴姓和房間號碼？

G : Yes. It's Witholt and I've been *staying in* Room #2305.

G：我叫威士歐特，住 2305 號房。

C : Just a moment, please. I'll check our room *availability* for the next three days. ……
Thank you for waiting, sir. I'm afraid our hotel is *fully booked for* the next week but *we may have cancellations*. Could you check with us again at 9:00 a.m. tomorrow morning?

C：請稍候，我查一下未來三天的空房間。……

先生，讓您久等了，下星期恐怕都已額滿，但是，可能會有人取消預約，請明天早上九點再問一次好嗎？

G : Well, what are the *chances* of getting a room? *If there are none available*, I'd like to make other arrangements.

G：唔，有沒有可能訂到房間呢？如果沒有空房間，我想另做安排。

C : I'm afraid I can't tell you that *at this stage*, sir. This is our *busy season*. If we cannot extend your booking, we will help you make a reservation with another hotel in the area.

C：這時候我恐怕還不能告訴您。現在是本店的旺季，如果不能延長您的登記，我們會幫您向本區別家旅館預約。

活 用 練 習

1 Your room has been booked for tomorrow. Would you mind changing rooms ?

您的房間明天已被訂走了。您介意換個房間嗎？

** **extend** 〔ɪk'stɛnd〕 *v.* 延長
　　moment 〔'momənt〕 *n.* 片刻；瞬間
　　availability 〔ə,velə'bɪlətɪ〕 *n.* 現有或可得之人或物
　　check with "諮詢；核對無誤"
　　arrangement 〔ə'rendʒmənt〕 *n.* 安排；佈置
　　stage 〔stedʒ〕 *n.* 時期

17 要求幫忙查詢電話號碼
Looking up a Telephone Number

── *對話精華* ───────────

◉ Could you *look* it *up* for me? 請幫我查一查好嗎?

◉ I'll contact *Directory Enquiries* and call you back.
我會和查號台聯絡並回電給您。

Dialogue : *G =* **Guest** 旅客　*C =* **Clerk** 職員

G : Operator, I'd like to contact a friend but I don't know his telephone number. Could you *look* it *up* for me?

G：總機,我想和一位朋友聯絡,但是我不知道他的電話號碼。請幫我查一查好嗎?

C : I see, sir. Do you know his *full name* and address?

C：我懂了,先生。您知道他的全名和地址嗎?

G : Yes. It's King Meng-fu and his address is 2F 16 Chin Shan South Road, Taipei.

G：是的,他叫金孟芙,地址是台北市金山南路16號2樓。

C : King Meng-fu of 2 F 16 Chin Shan South Road, Taipei.

C：台北市金山南路16號2樓的金孟芙。

G : That's it.

G：對的。

C : May I have your name and room number, please?

C：請問您貴姓和房間號碼？

G : Yes, it's Bellamy, and I'm in Room #2814.

G：我是貝勒米，住2814號房。

C : Thank you, sir. I will *contact Directory Enquiries* and *call* you *back*. ……
This is the Information Desk. Thank you for waiting, sir. Mr. King's number is 428 – 4530.

C：謝謝，先生。我會和查號台聯絡並回電給您。……

這裏是詢問台，讓您久等了，先生。金先生的電話號碼是 428 – 4530。

G : 428 – 4530. Thank you.

G：428 – 4530，謝謝。

C : You're welcome, sir.

C：不客氣。

** **operator** 〔'ɑpə,retɚ〕 *n.* 總機；接線生
   look up " 尋找；查閱 "
   Directory Enquiries 查號台

| A | B | | A is next to B. （A在B的隔壁）

| A | B | C | | B is between A and C. （B在A和C之間）

| D |
| E |

D is on top of E. （D在E上面）

E is under D. （E在D下面）

| H | | I |

H is along the hallway on the left.

（沿著走廊走下去，H在左手邊。）

I is along the hallway on the right.

（沿著走廊走下去，I在右手邊。）

| J | | K |

J is to the left. （向左轉就到J。）

K is to the right. （向右轉就到K。）

| L | | M |

L is at the end of the hallway to the left.

（L在走廊盡頭左轉。）

M is at the end of the hallway to the right.

（M在走廊盡頭右轉。）

| O |
| O |
| N |

N is through O. （穿過O就到N了。）

Go straight. （直走）

| Lobby |

This is the Lobby floor. （這是大廳所在的那層樓。）

| Banquet |

The Banquet Room is one floor down.

| Garage |

（宴會廳在底下一樓。）

The Garage is two floors down.

（車庫在底下二樓。）

Part 7

會計部門
The Front Cashier

1

結帳退宿手續
Check-out Procedure

〖 **對話精華** 〗

⚉ I want to *pay my bill*. 我要結帳。

⚉ Just a moment, please. The cashier will *have your bill ready* in a moment.
請稍等，出納員馬上會準備好您的帳單。

Dialogue : *C* = **Cashier** 出納員　*G* = **Guest** 旅客

C : Good morning, sir. May I help you?

C : 先生您早，需要我效勞嗎？

G : Yes, I'd like to ***settle my bill***.

G : 我想結帳。

C : Certainly sir. May I have your room key, please?

C : 好的，請把房間鑰匙給我好嗎？

G : Sure. Here you are.

G : 好的，在這兒。

C : Just a moment, please. I'll ***draw up*** your bill for you.……
Thank you for waiting, sir. ***Your bill totals*** NT$ 6,500.

C : 請等一下，我幫您結算帳單。
……
先生，讓您久等了，您的帳單總計台幣六千五百元。

G : That much! Would you mind letting me ***have a look at*** it?

G : 那麼多！你介不介意讓我看看呢？

C : Not at all, sir. Here you are.

C：不介意，您請看。

G : Thanks. Well, it seems to be right. How much is that *in dollars*, please?

G：謝謝，嗯，好像沒錯。請問合美金多少錢？

C : Just a moment, sir. I'll calculate that for you. *It comes to* 191 *dollars* 18 *cents at today's exchange rate*.

C：先生，請稍候，我幫您算算看。按今天的匯率折合美金一百九十一元十八分。

G : I see. O.K.

G：我知道了，好的。

C : How would you like to make the payment?

C：您預備如何付款？

G : *In cash*, please. Here you are.

G：付現金，錢在這兒。

C : Thank you, sir. NT$7000.⋯⋯ *Here is your change of* NT$500. Could you check it, please? Thank you for choosing our hotel. I hope you *enjoyed your stay*.

C：謝謝，台幣七千元。⋯⋯找您五百元零錢。請點點看好嗎？謝謝您選擇本店，但願您住得愉快。

** *draw up* "結算"　　**total** 〔'totḷ〕 *v*. 總計
have a look at "看看"　　**calculate** 〔'kælkjə,let〕 *v*. 計算
come to "總數達⋯"　　*exchange rate* （外幣的）匯率
change 〔tʃendʒ〕 *n*. 零錢

活 用 練 習

1 Shall I *draw up* your bill for you? 要我幫您結帳嗎?

2 Would you like a *breakdown* of the bill? 您的帳目要細分嗎?

3 I will *calculate* your bill for you. 我幫您計算帳單。

4 Your bill *comes (up) to* NT$6,000. 您的帳單合計六千元。

5 Your bill *stands at* NT$3,000. 您的帳單目前是三千元。
   (客人停留期間到櫃枱詢問時的回答)

6 Excuse me, sir, but I don't think that will be enough.
   對不起,我認為錢數不夠。

7 That will *cover the amount*. 那足夠支付總額了。

8 Here's your change and receipt. 這是您的零錢和收據。

9 Two hundred and forty-one dollars, forty-one cents.
   兩百四十一元四十一分。

10 Our *checkout time* is at noon but you used the room until
   6:00 p.m. I'm afraid that *for late checkout* we charge an
   extra 10% of the room rate. 本店的結帳時間在中午,而您使
   用房間到下午六點,我們恐怕要因延遲結帳而加收10%的房間費。

11 Hope to see you again soon. 希望很快再見到您。

12 *Is your baggage down* yet, sir? 您的行李還沒送下來嗎?

Could you check out after your bags have been brought down,
please? 請等行李送下來後再結帳好嗎?

⒁ Could you *leave the key with us* after your bags have been
brought down, please?
行李送下來之後請把鑰匙交還給我們好嗎?

** **breakdown** 〔'brek͵daʊn〕*n.* 分爲細目
　　cover 〔'kʌvɚ〕*v.* 足敷
　　amount 〔ə'maʊnt〕*n.* 總額;總數

▲ 旅館餐廳的招牌菜,也是使客人回味無窮、去而
　復返的要素之一。

2

由公司付帳的情形
Check-out by Company Account

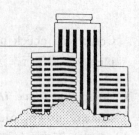

～ 〚對話精華〛 ～

◑ How would you like to make payment? 您要如何付款?

◑ My company will pay the bill (*pick up the tab*).
由我的公司付帳。

Dialogue: *C* = **Cashier** 出納員　*G* = **Guest** 旅客

C : How would you like to make payment?

C : 您要如何付款?

G : *On the company account*, please.

G : 請用公司帳戶。

C : May I know the name of your company, please?

C : 請問貴公司寶號?

G : Yes, it's G.N. Electrics, America.

G : 美國 G.N. 電器公司。

C : May I have two of your business cards, please?

C : 請給我兩張名片好嗎?

G : Why?

G : 為什麼要兩張呢?

C : *We'd like one for our files*, and one for accounts.

C : 我們要把一張放在檔案中, 一張附在帳單中。

G : I see. Here you are.

C : Just a moment, please. …
Thank you for waiting,
sir. Could you sign here,
please?

(*guest signs*)

C : Thank you. We hope to
welcome you again soon.

G：我懂了，拿去。

C：請稍後。……讓您久等了，
請在這兒簽名好嗎？

（客人簽名）

C：謝謝，我們希望很快再見到
您。

活 用 練 習

1 I'm afraid *we have no credit arrangements with your company*, sir. You may pay by any of these credit cards,
instead. 先生，我們與貴公司恐怕沒有信用貸款的協定，您可以改
用任何一種信用卡付款。

2 Mr. Yamada, Nihon Shoji *has arranged to pay your bill*.
山田先生，日本商事公司已安排支付您的帳單。

3 *May I have your signature, please*? 請簽名好嗎？

** *pick up the tab* "付帳"
account 〔ə'kaʊnt〕 *n.* 帳目；戶頭
electrics 〔ɪ'lɛktrɪks〕 *n.* 電器
business card 名片
file 〔faɪl〕 *n.* 檔案
signature 〔'sɪgnətʃɚ〕 *n.* 簽字

解釋信用卡限額
Explaining Credit Limits

〖 對話精華 〗

◉ The credit limit *set by* the Visa Card office is NT $10,000.

Visa 信用卡公司定的信用卡限額只有台幣一萬元。

◉ Would you like to *settle the difference* in cash?

您要用現金支付差額嗎？

Dialogue： *C* = **Cashier** 出納員　*G* = **Guest** 旅客

C： Your bill *totals* NT$12,000. How would you like to make the payment？

C：您的帳單總計台幣一萬二千元，您打算如何付款？

G： I'd like to **pay by credit card instead of in cash,** would that be all right？

G：我想用信用卡代替現金付款，可以嗎？

C： Certainly, sir. Which card would you like to use？

C：可以，您想用哪一種信用卡呢？

G： My Visa card.

G：我用 Visa 信用卡。

C： Do you have any other cards？

C：您有別的信用卡嗎？

G： No, just this one. Why？

G：只有這種，怎麼樣？

C : *The credit limit set by the Visa Card office is* NT$10,000. We need their permission to *extend credit over that amount.* Would you like to settle the difference in cash?

G : No, I'd prefer to pay the whole amount by credit.

C : Do you mind if we contact them and ask their permission?

G : No, *go ahead.* But it's the first time I've heard of a credit limit.

C : Just a moment, please. I'll call them for you. ……
Thank you for waiting, sir. They will call back very soon. Would you mind waiting until then?

C：Visa信用卡公司定的信用卡限額只有台幣一萬元，超出那個數目的信用款項，必須得到他們的允許。您要以現金支付差額嗎？

G：不，我寧願以信用卡支付全額。

C：您介不介意我們和他們聯絡，以請求他們的許可呢？

G：不，請便。但這是我第一次聽說信用卡有限額。

C：請稍候，我幫您打電話給他們。……
讓您久等了，他們馬上會回電。您介不介意等到那時候?

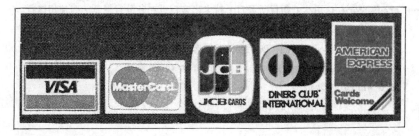

G : Well, *I'm in a hurry. How long will it take*?

G：哦，我在趕時間，要多久呢？

C : It should only take about five minutes, sir.

C：先生，應該只需要五分鐘。

G : O.K. I'll wait then.

G：好的，那麼我等。

　　　　　ⓒ　　　　　ⓒ　　　　　ⓒ

C : I'm very sorry to have kept you waiting, sir. The Visa office will extend credit for the whole amount.

C：對不起讓您久等，Visa公司願意把信用限額增加為全額。

G : *Well I should think so*.

G：想當然爾。

C : May I *take a print of* your card, please?

C：請讓我劃印您的信用卡好嗎？

G : Here you are and make it quick!

G：拿去，快點！

C : Certainly, sir. Could you sign here, please?

C：好的，先生。請在這兒簽名好嗎？

** *credit card* 信用卡（銀行所發行，持卡之客戶可在各分行提款，且使用該行支票償付貸款及工資，但每筆款有一定的限額）
credit limit 信用卡限額；商店等給予顧客之賒帳最高額
permission 〔pəˊmɪʃən〕*n.* 准許　　*prefer to* "寧願"
in a hurry "匆忙地"

4 標準滙兌手續

Standard Exchange Procedure

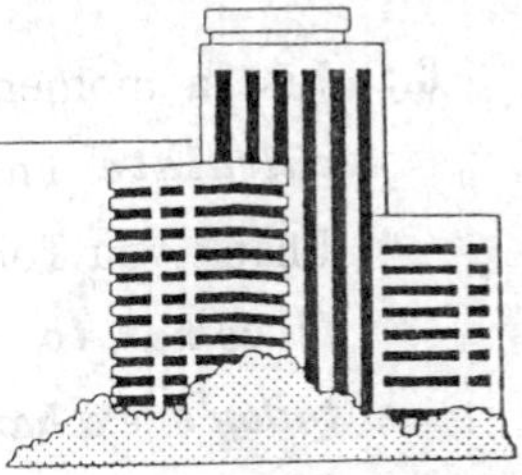

〖 對話精華 〗

- I'd like to *change* these U.S. dollars *into* NT dollars.
  我想把這些美元兌換成新台幣。
- It *comes to* NT$6,400 *at today's exchange rate.*
  按今天的匯率折合起來是新台幣六千四百元。

Dialogue : *C* = **Cashier** 出納員 *G* = **Guest** 旅客

C : Good morning, sir. May I help you?	C：先生您早，需要我效勞嗎？
G : Yes, I'd like to ***change*** these U.S. dollars ***into*** NT dollars.	G：我想把這些美元兌換成新台幣。
C : Certainly, sir. Could you ***fill out*** this form, please?	C：好的，先生，請填寫這張表格好嗎？
G : Here you are.	G：填好了。
C : Thank you, sir. You would like to ***change*** US$200 ***into*** NT dollars. Is that right?	C：謝謝您，先生，您想把二百美元換成台幣，對不對？
G : Yes, that's right.	G：是的。

C : Just a moment, please. I'll **calculate** that for you. Thank you for waiting, sir. **It comes to** NT$6,400 **at today's exchange rate**.

C：請稍候。我幫您計算一下。

先生，讓您久等了，按今天的匯率折合起來是新台幣六千四百元。

G : I see. Here you are.

G：我明白了，給你。

C : And here are your NT dollars. Thank you, sir. Have a nice day.

C：這是您的新台幣，謝謝，祝您愉快。

活 用 練 習

1 Would you like to change some money? 您要匯兌一些錢嗎？

2 We accept **traveller's checks**. 我們接受旅行支票。

3 I'm afraid we don't accept **non-convertible currency**, sir. Could you change it at a Foreign Exchange Bank?
先生，我們恐怕不接受未兌現的貨幣，您到外匯銀行兌換好嗎？

** NT$ = New Taiwan dollar 新台幣
exchange〔ɪks'tʃendʒ〕v. 兌換　n.（外幣的）滙率
check〔tʃɛk〕n. 支票
non-convertible〔͵nɑnkən'vɝtəbḷ〕a. 未兌換的
currency〔'kɝənsɪ〕n. 通貨（硬幣或紙幣）

5 説明夜間滙兌限額
Explaining the Night Change Limits

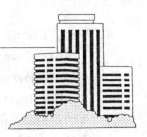

《對話精華》

● *We have a change limit of* 500 *U.S. dollars* between 9:00 p.m. and 8:00 a.m. due to the bank business hours. 由於銀行營業時間的關係，在晚上九點到早上八點之間，我們定有五百美元的滙兌限制。

● Can't you *make an exception* for me?
你們不能為我破例一次嗎？

Dialogue : *C* = **Cashier** 出納員　*G* = **Guest** 旅客

C : Good evening, ma'am. May I help you?

C：女士，晚安，能為您效勞嗎?

G : Yes, I'd like to change some money, please.

G：請幫我兌換一些錢。

C : Certainly ma'am. How much would you like to change?

C：好的，您預備兌換多少呢？

G : Let's see. I'll need about six hundred U.S. dollars.

G：我看看。我需要六百美元左右。

C : We have a *change limit* of 500 U.S. dollars between 9:00 p.m. and 8:00 a.m. *due to the bank business hours*.

C：由於銀行營業時間的關係，在晚上九點到早上八點之間，我們定有五百美元的滙兌限制。

G : Well, I'll be leaving at 7:30 a.m. *on an all-day tour* tomorrow and I'll need at least that much. We're going to Yingko and I want to buy a lot of *ceramics*. I won't be anywhere near a bank. *Can't you make an exception for me*?

G：是這樣的，我明天上午七點半離開，去參加一個全天的旅行團，而我至少需要那麼多錢。我們要到鶯歌，我要買許多陶器，附近不會有銀行，你們不能爲我破例一次嗎？

C : I'm afraid, ma'am, that we have to *place a limit on exchange for the benefit of* all our guests. If we change large amounts, our cash supply *runs out* and we are unable to *oblige* our other guests.

C：女士，恐怕不行，爲了全體顧客的利益，我們必須設定匯兌的限額，如果我們兌換大額款項，致使現金外流，我們就無法服務其他客人了。

G : Well, why do you keep such a small amount *in the first place*?

G：那麼，首先，你們爲什麼只保留這麼小筆的款額呢？

C : We *restrict* the amount of cash *kept at night for security reasons*.

C：我們是基於安全的理由而在晚間限定現金的款額。

G : I see. Well, I suppose it can't be helped.

G：我懂了。那麼，我猜是沒輒了。

C : Why don't you ask the tour guide to *stop* at a major branch of a bank *en route to get exchange*?

C：您何不請導遊半途在銀行主要的分行停車，以便匯兌呢?

G : That's a good idea. I'll do that.

G：好主意，我就這麼做吧。

活 用 練 習

① The Exchange Counter will be open from 8:00 a.m. tomorrow. Could you change your money there?

匯兌櫃枱從明天早上八點開始營業，您到那裏換錢好嗎?

** *due to* = *because of* "由於"
   ceramics 〔sə'ræmɪks〕 *n*. 陶器
   exception 〔ɪk'sɛpʃən〕 *n*. 例外
   benefit 〔'bɛnəfɪt〕 *n*. 利益
   oblige 〔ə'blaɪdʒ〕 *v*. 應命；施以恩惠
   restrict 〔rɪ'strɪkt〕 *v*. 限制
   security 〔sɪ'kjʊrətɪ〕 *n*. 安全
   tour guide 導遊
   major branch 主要的分行
   en route (= *on the way*) "在途中"

6 保險櫃
Safety Deposit Box

⊛ I'd like to use a *safety deposit box*. 我想使用保險櫃。

⊛ Would you like to use it *until May 20th*？
您預備使用到五月二十日嗎？

Dialogue : *C* = **Clerk** 職員　　*G* = **Guest** 旅客

C : Good evening, ma'am. May I help you.

C : 女士，晚安，能爲您效勞嗎？

G : Yes. I'd like to use a *safety deposit box*.

G : 我想使用保險櫃。

C : Certainly, ma'am. Could you *fill out* this form, please?

C : 好的，請填寫這張表格好嗎?

G : Here you are.

G : 填好了。

C : Thank you, ma'am. Would you like to use it until May 20th?

C : 謝謝，您預備使用到五月二十日嗎？

G : Yes.

G : 是的。

C： This way, please. Your box number is 520.

C： 請跟我來，您的櫃子是 520 號。

G： Thank you.

G： 謝謝。

活 用 練 習

1 How big is the object？該物品有多大？

2 I'm afraid you can only use this *until your check-out date*.
恐怕您只能使用本櫃到結帳那天。

3 *Will it fit into this size of box*？
東西適合擺進這種大小的櫃子嗎？

4 Have you *finished with* the box？您不須再使用這個櫃子嗎？
Will you be using the box any longer？您還要再使用這個櫃子嗎？

5 Would you like to *deposit* or *withdraw* something？
您要存放或提出什麼東西？

6 Could you keep this key carefully, please. *There is no spare*.
The box can only be opened with these keys. 請小心保存這支鑰匙好嗎？我們沒有備用的鑰匙，而這櫃子只有這些鑰匙可以打開。

7 If you would like to use the contents during the period of use, *please come here in person*. After confirming your signature, we will open the box. 使用本櫃期間，您若想取用裏面的東西，請親自前來。待確認您的簽名之後，我們才開櫃。

** **deposit** 〔dɪˈpɑzɪt〕*v*. 儲存；寄託
　　withdraw 〔wɪðˈdrɔ〕*v*. 取回；收回　　**spare** 〔spɛr〕*adj*. 備用的；剩餘的
　　content 〔ˈkɑntɛnt〕*n*. (容器等)內部所容之物　　***in person*** " 親自 "
　　confirm 〔kənˈfɝm〕*v*. 確認；證實　　**signature** 〔ˈsɪgnətʃɚ〕*n*. 簽字

如果旅客使用旅行支票（ *traveller's check* ）、信用卡（ *credit card* ）或私人支票（ *personal check* ）以代替現金付帳時，要特別注意以下十點：

1. 旅行支票下欄必須**當面副署**（ *counter signed* ），且上下兩欄簽字式樣必須一致，以證明他是眞正的持有人。

2. 若誤將旅行支票簽名寫在**抬頭人**的位置上，則旅館無法兌換現金。此時必須請旅客另換一張，或請他在下欄（ *counter sign* ）的位置上補簽並加以背書。

3. 信用卡付帳時，須**核對**該卡之**有效日期**，提早或過期均不可接受。

4. 收帳單（ *Charge Form* ）及信用卡放入印號機內刷印時，寧可多用一張，切**不可印兩次**，因號碼印不清楚則視同廢紙。

5. 以信用卡付款時，要填好金額、日期，請旅客在帳單上簽名。

6. 大來信用卡公司（ *Diner's Club* ）也發行地方性信用卡，指定在特殊地區（如南美、西歐…）方可使用。一定要注意印有 *World-wide* 的才可以接受。

7. **信用卡的簽帳金額都有明確的限制**，如果超過，應事先電告發卡公司，申請特許。

8. 私人支票或與旅館關係不深的公司行號所開出的支票，除非由主管批准，否則都應婉拒，請他以 現金付款 。

9. 收到支票時經手人應背書，並寫上出票人電話或地址備查。

10. 收到支票時，應注意**日期**（年底時尤須特別注意年份）、**金額、抬頭人、出票人簽章**等各項有無錯誤或遺漏。

Part 8

客房管理部
Housekeeping

1

説明洗衣服務時間
Explaining Laundry Service Hours

《 對話精華 》

◐ I'd like to know about your laundry service hours.
我想知道你們洗衣服務的時間。

◐ If your laundry is received before 10:00 a.m., *we will deliver it to your room by* 10:00 p.m. *the same day.* 如果在早上十點以前接到您送洗的衣物，我們會在當天下午十點以前送回您房裏。

Dialogue： *H* = **Housekeeper** 旅館客房管理部管理員　　*G* = **Guest** 旅客

H： Good morning. Housekeeping. May I help you?

G：客房管理部，您早。需要我效勞嗎？

G： Yes, I'd like to know about your laundry service hours.

H：我想知道你們洗衣服務的時間。

H： If your laundry is received before 10:00 a.m., *we will deliver it to your room by* 10:00 p.m. *the same day.* If we receive it before 3:00 p.m., we'll get it back to you by noon the next day, sir.

G：先生，如果在早上十點以前接到您送洗的衣物，我們會在當天下午十點以前送回您房裏。如果是在下午三點以前收到，則要到第二天中午以前才送回去。

G : *What are your rates*?

G：怎麼收費呢？

H : That rate chart is contained in the stationery folder in your dresser drawer, sir.

H：先生，費率表包括在您化妝台抽屜裏的文具摺疊小冊子上。

G : I see.... Well, would you please send someone to room 604 to *pick up* some laundry for me?

G：我知道了……哦，請派個人到604房幫我收一些送洗的衣服，好嗎？

H : Yes, sir. The roommaid will be there in a few minutes, sir.

H：好的，先生。女侍幾分鐘之內就會到那裏。

G : Thank you.

G：謝謝。

H : You're welcome, sir.

H：不客氣，先生。

活 用 練 習

① For laundry service, dial 6 and *you will get housekeeping*.
若需要洗衣服務，請撥6和客房管理部連絡。

② We will deliver it to your room by tomorrow noon.
我們會在明天中午以前送回您房裏。

③ If you are *in a hurry* we have a two hour quick service.
如果您急著要，我們有兩個小時的快速服務。

④ ***There is an extra charge of*** 50% for quick service.
快速服務需要額外付50％的費用。

** **chart** 〔tʃɑrt〕 *n.* 圖；表
contain 〔kən'ten〕 *v.* 包含
stationery 〔'steʃən,ɛrɪ〕 *n.* 文具
folder 〔'foldɚ〕 *n.* 摺疊的小冊子
dresser 〔'drɛsɚ〕 *n.* 化妝台

△各種遊樂設施，可使客人達到最高遊憩目的。

2

洗衣服務受理程序
Laundry Reception Procedure

〚對話精華〛

▲ I'd like this sweater washed *by hand in cold water.*
這件毛衣要用冷水手洗。

▲ Is this for *pressing* only? 這件只要燙平嗎？

Dialogue： *H =* **Houseman** 客房服務員　*G =* **Guest** 旅客

H : Housekeeping. May I come in?

H：客房管理部，可以進來嗎？

G : Yes. I'd like to have this laundry done, please?

G：可以，這些衣服要送洗。

H : Certainly, sir. Could you fill out the *laundry form*, please?

H：好的，先生，請填寫洗衣單好嗎？

G : Where is it?

G：在哪兒？

H : It's in the *drawer* of the writing desk.

H：在寫字枱的抽屜裏。

G : Fine. May I use your pen?

G：好的，可以借用你的筆嗎？

H : Certainly, sir. Here you are.

H：當然可以，請便。

G: Thanks. Oh, and *I don't want these shirts starched*.

G：謝謝。對了，這些襯衫不要用漿的。

H: *No starch*. I understand, sir.

H：不漿，我了解，先生。

G: Yes, and I'd like this sweater washed *by hand* in cold water. *It might shrink otherwise*.

G：這件毛衣要用冷水手洗，否則可能會縮水。

H: By hand in cold water. I understand.

H：用冷水手洗，我明白了。

G: When will it be ready?

G：什麼時候可以洗好？

H: We will deliver them tomorrow evening *around* 6:00 p.m.

H：我們明天下午六點左右會送過來。

G: Fine. Thanks a lot.

G：好的，謝謝。

活用練習

1 I'll send someone immediately. 我立刻派人過去。

2 Is this for washing, ma'am? 女士，這是要清洗的嗎？

3 Is this *for pressing only*, ma'am? 女士，這只要燙平嗎？

4 The laundry forms and bags are *in the top right-hand drawer* of the writing desk.
洗衣單和洗衣袋在寫字枱的右邊第一個抽屜裏。

5 The Front Desk will handle your laundry, sir. *Could you put it in the laundry bag provided* and leave it at the Front Desk, please? 先生，櫃枱會處理您送洗的衣物，請放入備好的洗衣袋並交給櫃枱好嗎？

** **laundry** 〔'lɔndrɪ〕 *n*. 送洗的衣服
drawer 〔drɔr〕 *n*. 抽屜
starch 〔startʃ〕 *v*. 漿硬（衣服等）
sweater 〔'swɛtɚ〕 *n*. 毛衣
shrink 〔ʃrɪŋk〕 *v*. 縮水；收縮
otherwise 〔'ʌðɚ,waɪz〕 *adv*. 否則
press 〔prɛs〕 *v*. 熨
handle 〔'hændḷ〕 *v*. 處理
provide 〔prə'vaɪd〕 *v*. 預備

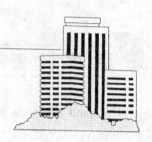

逾時送洗衣物
Too Late for That Day's Laundry

〖對話精華〗

● I'm afraid *it's too late for* today's laundry.
　現在恐怕已過了今天的洗衣時間。

● That's O.K. *It's not urgent.* 沒關係，並不急著要。

Dialogue： *G* = **Guest** 旅客　*H* = **Housekeeper** 管理員

G : Hello. Is this Housekeeping?

G：喂，是客房管理部嗎？

H : Speaking. May I help you?

H：是的，需要我效勞嗎？

G : Yes. Could you send someone to *pick up my laundry*, please?

G：請派人來取我要送洗的衣物好嗎？

H : I'm afraid *it's too late for today's laundry*, ma'am. We can deliver it tomorrow around 6:00 p.m.

H：女士，現在恐怕已過了今天的洗衣時間，要到明天傍晚六點左右才會送回來。

G : That's O.K. *It's not urgent.*

G：沒關係，並不急著要。

H : Could you leave it on the bed, if you are going out, ma'am?

H：女士，如果您要出門，請把衣服放在床上好嗎？

G : Sure. *I'll do that.*　　　　　　G：當然好，我會照辦。

H : Thank you, ma'am. Good-　　　H：謝謝您，再見
bye.

G : Goodbye.　　　　　　　　　　G：再見。

活 用 練 習

① *It will be ready by* 6:00 p.m. this evening.
今晚六點以前可以洗好。

② There is no laundry service on Sundays.
星期日沒有洗衣服務。

③ Laundry received before 10:00 a.m. will be returned by 6:00
p.m. on the same day.
上午十點以前收取送洗衣物，當天下午六點送回。

④ We have a *special four-hour service.* 我們有四小時的特別服務。

⑤ We will deliver it within 4 hours at a 50% *extra charge.*
我們可以在四小時內送回，但要增收 50% 的費用。

** urgent〔'ɝdʒənt〕*adj.* 緊急的
ready〔'rɛdɪ〕*adj.* 準備好的

4

需要乾洗時
Dry-cleaned

〖 對話精華 〗

◉ *I'd like this garment dry-cleaned*, please.
這件衣服要乾洗。

◉ I'm sorry but we don't have the special equipment
necessary. 抱歉，我們沒有所需的特別設備。

◉ *That's not your fault*. 那不是你們的錯。

Dialogue : *G* = **Guest** 旅客　*H* = **Houseman** 客房服務員

G : I'd like this garment *dry-cleaned*, please.

G：這件衣服要乾洗。

H : I'm afraid we cannot launder *embroidered items*, ma'am.

H：女士，我們恐怕不能洗繡花類的衣服。

G : Why not?

G：爲什麼不能。

H : We do not have the *facilities* and we cannot *take responsibility for* any damage.

H：我們沒有這項設備，而且如果有任何破損，我們負不起責任。

G : Well, O.K. But what about this coat?

G：好吧，那這件外套呢？

H : I'm sorry but we do not have the *special equipment* necessary.

H：抱歉，我們沒有所需的特別設備。

G : That's a nuisance!

G：那眞是討厭。

H : I'm very sorry we couldn't help you, ma'am.

H：女士，非常抱歉，我們無能爲力。

G : *That's not your fault.*

G：那不是你們的錯。

** **garment** 〔'gɑrmənt〕 *n.* 衣服；外衣
   dry-cleaned 乾洗的
   embroidered 〔ɪm'brɔɪdə·d〕 *adj.* 刺繡的
   facilities 〔fə'sɪlətɪz〕 *n.* (*pl.*) 設備
   responsibility 〔rɪ,spɑnsə'bɪlətɪ〕 *n.* 責任
   equipment 〔ɪ'kwɪpmənt〕 *n.* 設備
   nuisance 〔'njusn̩s〕 *n.* 討厭的人或事物

補綴和去污
Mending & Stain Removal

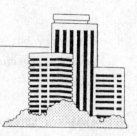

《 對話精華 》

❀ Do you have *a mending service* for clothes?
你們有縫補衣服的服務嗎?

❀ Yes, we can mend them. 是的,我們可以縫補。

Dialogue : *G* = **Guest** 旅客　　*H* = **Houseman** 客房服務員

G : Do you have *a mending service* for clothes?

H : Pardon me.

G : A mending service. I'd like these socks *darned*.

H : I see, sir. Yes, we can mend them.

G : There's this jacket, too. It has a tear in it.

H : I'm sorry, sir. *We can mend a seam but not a hole*.

G:你們有縫補衣服的服務嗎?

H:原諒我(我不了解您的意思)。

G:縫補服務,我想補這些襪子。

H:我懂了。是的,我們可以縫補。

G:這件夾克也要,上面有個破洞。

H:先生,對不起,我們只補裂縫而不補破洞。

G : There's also a *stain* on this jacket. I'd like it *removed* before it's dry-cleaned.

G：還有這件夾克上有污點，我想在乾洗前去掉它。

H : May I see it, please?

H：請讓我看看好嗎？

G : Yes, here you are.

G：好的，在這兒。

H : What kind of stain is it, sir?

H：是哪一種污點呢？

G : I *spilled* some soy sauce *on* it.

G：上面潑到了醬油。

H : We will *do our best* to remove the stain but we cannot *guarantee* the result.

H：我們會盡力除去這個污點，但無法保證結果如何。

G : That's O.K. How long do you think it will take?

G：沒關係，你認為要花多少時間呢？

H : I'm not sure, sir, but I *will check with the Laundry* and let you know.

H：我不確定，但是我會向洗衣部查詢並通知您。

G : Fine. I'd like it *as soon as possible*.

G：好的，希望儘快。

活用練習

① I'm afraid we couldn't remove the stain.
　我們恐怕無法去掉這污點。

② We can only do (*undertake*) **simple mending.**
　我們只受理簡單的縫補。

**　**mend** 〔mɛnd〕*v*. 修補
　pardon 〔'pɑrdn̩〕*v*. 原諒
　darn 〔dɑrn〕*v*. 縫補；補綴
　tear 〔tɛr〕*n*. 破處；磨損
　seam 〔sim〕*n*. 裂縫
　stain 〔sten〕*n*. 污跡
　remove 〔rɪ'muv〕*v*. 除去
　spill 〔spɪl〕*v*. 潑灑
　soy sauce 醬油
　do one's best "盡力"
　guarantee 〔,gærən'ti〕*v*. 擔保

6

衣物分送錯誤
Mis-delivery

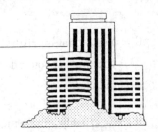

〰〰〰〰〰〰〰

『對話精華』

◈ May I have the *misdelivered* items, please?
請把送錯的衣物交給我好嗎？

◈ Sure, I'll *get them for you.* 好的，我拿給你。

◈ We are very sorry for the *inconvenience.*
很抱歉使您不方便。

〰〰〰〰〰〰〰

Dialogue :　*H* = **Housekeeper** 管理員　　*G* = **Guest** 旅客

H : Housekeeping. May I help you?

H：客房管理部，需要我效勞嗎?

G : Yes. The maid delivered some laundry to my room **but it's not mine**!

G：女侍送了一些衣物到我房裏，但那並不是我的!

H : I'm sorry, ma'am. We will send someone immediately.

H：對不起，女士。我立刻派人過去。

(Goes to room)

（前往客房）

H : Housekeeping. I've brought your laundry. Is this yours, ma'am?

H：客房管理部，我把您送洗的衣物拿來了。女士，這是您的吧？

G : Yes, that's right. Could
you put it on the bed,
please?

G：是的，這就對了。請放在我
的床上好嗎？

H : Certainly, ma'am. May I
have *the misdelivered
items*, please?

H：當然好，女士，請把送錯的
衣物交給我好嗎？

G : Sure, I'll get them for
you.

G：好的，我拿給你。

H : Thank you, ma'am. We
are very sorry for the
inconvenience?

H：謝謝，女士。很抱歉使您不
方便。

G : *That's all right.*

G：沒關係。

** **maid** 〔med〕 *n.* 女侍
 immediately 〔ɪˈmidɪɪtlɪ〕 *adv.* 立刻
 certainly 〔ˈsɝtn̩lɪ〕 *adv.* 當然地
 misdelivered 〔ˌmɪsdɪˈlɪvɚd〕 *adj.* 誤送
 item 〔ˈaɪtəm〕 *n.* 項目
 incovenience 〔ˌɪnkənˈvinjəns〕 *n.* 不便

7

送洗衣物受損時
When Laundry Is Damaged

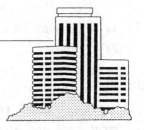

〖 **對話精華** 〗

● I sent a sweater to the Laundry *but it's come back badly shrunk.*

　　我有一件毛衣拿去送洗，但是送回來後嚴重縮水。

● We'll *refund the cost* of the laundry and the new sweater. 我們會退還新毛衣和洗衣的費用。

Dialogue : *H* = **Housekeeper** 管家　　*G* = **Guest** 旅客

H : Housekeeping. May I help you?

H : 客房管理部，需要我效勞嗎?

G : Yes. I sent a sweater to the Laundry but it's **come back badly shrunk.**

G : 我有一件毛衣拿去送洗，但是送回來後嚴重縮水。

H : We're very sorry, ma'am. I'll send someone imme-diately.

H : 女士，非常抱歉，我立刻派人過去。

　　(*Goes to room*)

　　(前往客房)

H : Housekeeping. May I come in?

H : 客房管理部，我可以進來嗎?

G : Yes. Look at this sweater. *It's ruined*.

G：可以，看看這件毛衣，報銷了。

H : We're very sorry, ma'am. Could you buy a *replacement* here and give us the receipt? We will *refund the cost* of the laundry and the new sweater.

H：女士，非常抱歉，您在此地買件代替品，並把收據交給我們好嗎？我們會退還新毛衣和洗衣的費用。

G : Listen, I won't have time to buy a new one, and *in any case* I'm sure I won't be able *to find one my size*!

G：聽著，我沒有時間去買新的，而且無論如何，我相信無法找到適合我穿的尺碼！

H : Could you buy a replacement in your home country and send us the receipt? We will send you *a bank draft for the amount*.

H：您可以在貴國買到代替品，並把收據寄給我們嗎？我們會用銀行匯票把錢寄給您。

G : I should hope so!

G：就只能這樣啦！

H : Could you *fill out* this form *with* your name and forwarding address? We are very sorry for the inconvenience.

H：請在表格上填寫您的大名和郵寄地址好嗎？抱歉使您不方便。

活用練習

⬜1 Would you like to *speak to* the Manager?
您要和經理談談嗎？

** **shrunk**〔ʃrʌŋk〕*v.*（shrink 的過去分詞）縮水；收縮
ruin〔'ruɪn〕*v.* 毀壞
replacement〔rɪ'plesmənt〕*n.* 代替的人或物
refund〔rɪ'fʌnd〕*v.* 償還
in any case　" 無論如何 "
bank draft　銀行滙票
forward〔'fɔrwəd〕*v.* 轉遞；轉寄
manager〔'mænɪdʒə〕*n.* 經理

8
結帳後有物品遺留在房裡
Checking out But Leaving Some Items in the Room

〖 對話精華 〗

◓ I *must have left* my coat in my room.
　我的外套一定是留在房間裏了。

◓ Could you come to Room #3720 now? *We'll wait for you there*?
　　請現在到3720號房來好嗎？我們會在那裏等您。

Dialogue： *H* = **Housekeeper** 管理員　*G* = **Guest** 旅客

H： Housekeeping. May I help you?

H：客房管理部，能為您效勞嗎？

G： Yes. I've just checked out but I think I must have *left* my coat in my room.

G：是的，我剛剛結完帳，但我想我的外套一定是留在房間裏了。

H： May I have your name and room number, please?

H：請問您貴姓及房間號碼？

G： Yes. It's Wilson and I was in Room #3720.

G：我是威爾森，住3720號房。

H： Could you come to Room #3720 now? We'll *wait for* you there.

H：請現在到3720號房來好嗎？我們會在那裏等您。

G : O.K. I'll be there *right away.*

(*Goes to room*)

H : Excuse me, sir, but are you Mr. Wilson?

G : That's right.

H : *Could you fill out this request slip,* please?

G : Sure. Here you are.

H : I'm sorry, sir, but may I see some *identification,* please?

G : Here's my *passport.*

H : Thank you, sir. (*Opens door*). *After you,* sir.

G : I think I must have left it in the closet. Ah yes, *here it is*!

G：好的，我馬上過去。

（ 到房間去 ）

H：先生，對不起，您是威爾森先生嗎？

G：是的。

H：請填寫這張申請單好嗎？

G：好的，填好了。

H：對不起，可不可以看看您的證件？

G：這是我的護照。

H：先生，謝謝，（ 開門 ）您先請。

G：我想一定是留在衣櫥裏。嗯，對了，在這兒！

活用練習

① We have checked our *Lost and Found List* but I'm afraid your glasses did not appear on it.

　我們已查過失物招領單，但是您的眼鏡恐怕並未被記錄在內。

② Could you *fill out* the Lost Property Form, please?

　請填寫財物遺失單好嗎？

③ We will contact you if it is *located*.

　如果找到了，我們會與您聯絡。

** *wait for* " 等待 "

request 〔rɪˈkwɛst〕 *n*. 請求

identification 〔aɪ,dɛntəfəˈkeʃən〕 *n*. 證件

passport 〔ˈpæs,port〕 *n*. 護照

closet 〔ˈklɑzɪt〕 *n*. 衣櫥

appear 〔əˈpɪr〕 *v*. 出現

property 〔ˈprɑpətɪ〕 *n*. 財產；所有物

locate 〔loˈket〕 *v*. 尋出…的位置

要結帳退宿時，務必檢查一下東西是否都帶了。

　　有經驗的旅客會在遷出前一兩個小時，或提早在前一天晚上臨睡前先結帳，以免臨去匆匆，容易發生錯誤。但大部份旅客則在離去前，將行李送至大廳時才結帳，若人數多時容易造成擁擠的現象，通常尖峯時間約在早上八點至十點左右。

　　旅客結帳時，收銀員必須查看帳卡上的房號和姓名有無錯誤，並**把姓名唸出來**（如Mr. John Smith），以避免因帳卡放錯位置而發生付錯帳單的情形。並查清楚是否還有未登記上去的簽單（如早餐、洗衣費、三溫暖等），或是否有附著其他應辦事項的紙條，譬如該名旅客的帳單由某公司付款，或另一旅客的帳單由他支付等。

　　旅客在上午遷出時，應注意其早餐的帳單是否已記入帳卡中，如果帳卡上並未記入當天的新帳，可以問對方：

Have you had your breakfast, sir？
—— Yes, I have.
Did you sign any check today？
—— Yes, I did.　No, I paid in cash.

　　旅客結帳後，應將帳卡放在帳卡機（Billing Machine）上，打上**Paid in Full**，使餘額變成零，然後將第一聯蓋印後，連同記帳憑證，交給旅客作收據，第二聯轉送會計組作為核帳及備查之用。並將金額填入現金收入日報（*Cash Receipt Report*），如果旅客不是付現金，則請旅客或代旅客付帳之公司或私人，在帳卡上簽名，將兩聯移送會計組，派收帳員收帳。登記卡則在背後打上遷出時間，連同鑰匙移交給接待人員列為空房。

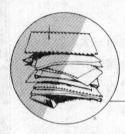

Standard Lost Property Letter

Dear Mr. Smith,

Thank you for your letter of May 8, 2008. We hope that you enjoyed your stay with us.

Regarding the pair of trousers and the belt which you think you might have left in your room, we regret that despite a diligent search by our housekeeping staff, we have been unable to locate them.

All items which have been lost or left behind at the hotel are immediately deposited with our Housekeeping Department, which enters them on their records and will forward them to the owner on request. We have checked the lists for May 27— May 30, but unfortunately neither your trousers nor your belt were among the many articles received at that time. We sincerely regret, therefore, that we are unable to assist you.

We hope that this will not have marred your memories of your stay with us and we look forward to welcoming you on any future visits you might make to Taipei.

Sincerely yours,

回覆詢問遺失物品的信函

史密斯先生：

感謝您 2008 年 5 月 8 號的來信，但願您在此與我們共度了快樂的時光。

有關您認為可能遺失在房裏的長褲及皮帶，很遺憾，儘管客房管理部人員仔細檢查過，仍舊無法找到。

遺失或遺忘在旅館的物品，向來都是立刻存放到我們的客房管理部，填入記錄表，並交還前來詢問的失主。我們已查過 5 月 27 日～30 日的記錄表，很不幸地，您的長褲和皮帶並不在該時間收到的眾多遺失物品之中。因此，非常抱歉我們無能為力。

我們希望這件事不會損傷您停留本店的印象，並期待您未來若前來台北，再度光臨本飯店。

敬上

** **regarding** 〔rɪˈgardɪŋ〕 *prep.* 關於   **trousers** 〔ˈtraʊzəz〕 *n.* 褲
diligent 〔ˈdɪlədʒənt〕 *adj.* 細心的   **staff** 〔stæf〕 *n.* 人員
mar 〔mar〕 *v.* 損傷

請求清理房間
Asking to Clean the Room

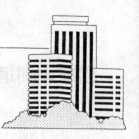

『對話精華』

◉ I'm sorry to *disturb* you, but we'd like to clean the room. 抱歉打擾您，我們想清理這個房間。

◉ Well, I'm *a bit tied up* at the moment.
哦，我現在有點事情。

◉ Can't *you come back* later? 你們等會再來好嗎？

Dialogue : *H* = **House maid** 女服務員　　*G* = **Guest** 旅客

H : Housekeeping. May I come in?

H：客房管理部，我可以進來嗎？

G : Yes, *what is it* ?

G：可以，有什麼事啊？

H : I'm sorry to *disturb* you, sir, but we'd like to clean the room. May we do it now?

H：先生，抱歉打擾您，我們想清理這個房間，現在可以嗎？

G : Well, I'm *a bit tied up* at the moment.

G：哦，我現在有點事情，等會再來好嗎？

H : What time would be convenient, sir ?

H：先生，什麼時候方便呢？

G : Let's see. Could you come again *around* 5:00 p.m.?

G：我想想看。你們下午五點左右再來好嗎？

H : I'm afraid *no cleaning can be done* between 4:30 and 6:00 p.m., sir. May we come *between* 6:30 and 7:30 p.m.?

H：下午四點半到六點恐怕無法清理，我們下午六點半到七點半之間來好嗎？

G : I guess so. I'll be out then anyway.

G：我想可以，無論如何那時我會出去。

活 用 練 習

① May we clean your room now, sir?
先生，我們現在可以清理您的房間嗎？

② *Shall we come back later*, sir? 先生，要我們等會兒再來嗎？

③ I'm sorry, but could you wait *another* 30 minutes, please?
對不起，請再等三十分鐘好嗎？

④ We will come and clean your room immediately.
我們會立刻來清理您的房間。

** disturb〔dɪ'stɝb〕*v.* 打擾
tied up = *busy* "忙碌"
at the moment "現在；目前"

10

借用電器設備時
Borrowing Equipment from Housekeeping

〖 對話精華 〗

◉ Do you have *a converter* I could use?
你們有我可以使用的變頻器嗎？

◉ We can lend you *a hair dryer* instead.
我們可以改成借您吹風機。

Dialogue： *G* = Guest 旅客　*H* = Housekeeper 管理員

G： Is this Housekeeping?

G：客房管理部嗎？

H： *Speaking.* May I help you?

H：是的，需要我效勞嗎？

G： Yes, I'd like to use my *hair dryer* but it's 220 volts. Do you have a *converter* I could use?

G：我想使用我的吹風機，但它是 220 伏特的，你們有我可以使用的變頻器嗎？

H： Yes, we do, ma'am. But I'm afraid another guest is using it now. *We can lend you a hair dryer instead.*

H：有的，但現在恐怕另有客人在使用，我們可以改成借您吹風機。

G： Fine. Could you bring it soon?

G：也好，請立刻送過來好嗎？

H : Certainly, ma'am. I'll send someone immediately.　　H：好的，女士。我立刻派人送過去。

活 用 練 習

1 You may use 100 and 110 volt *appliances* in your room.

您可以在房間使用 100 及 110 伏特的電器。

2 If the appliance has a higher *voltage*, could you use it *with a converter*, please？

若有電壓量較大的器具請配合變頻器使用好嗎？

3 I'm afraid guests are not allowed to use *irons* or *electric heaters* in their rooms.

客人恐怕不准在房間裏使用熨斗或電熱器。

4 We will bring a baby bed immediately.

我們立刻送嬰兒床過來。

5 We wondered if you had finished using the hair dryer. Another guest would like to use it.

我們想知道吹風機用好了沒？有別的客人要用。

** *hair dryer* 吹風機；整髮器　　**volt** 〔volt〕 *n.* 伏特
　converter 〔kən'vɜtə〕 *n.* 變頻器　　**appliance** 〔ə'plaɪəns〕 *n.* 器具
　voltage 〔'voltɪdʒ〕 *n.* 電壓量　　**iron** 〔'aɪən〕 *n.* 電熨斗
　electric heater 電熱器　　**wonder** 〔'wʌndə〕 *v.* 想知道
　finish 〔'fɪnɪʃ〕 *v.* 結束；完成

11 客房服務

Room Service

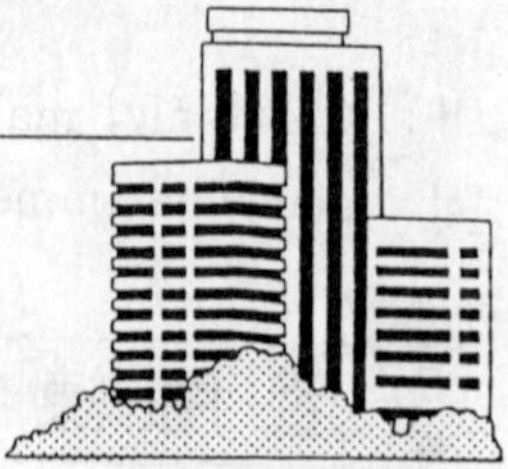

『對話精華』

- Can you *send up* two bottles of Coca-Cola, please?
  請送兩瓶可口可樂上來好嗎？
- We don't *sell drinks* in Housekeeping.
  客房管理部不賣飲料。

Dialogue: *G*= **Guest** 旅客 *H*= **Housekeeper** 管理員

G: Can you ***send up*** two bottles of Coca-Cola, please?	G: 請送兩瓶可口可樂上來好嗎?
H: We do not sell drinks in Housekeeping, ma'am. Could you dial 2 for Room Service, please?	H: 客房管理部不賣飲料，請撥2線到客房服務部好嗎？
G: I'm ***in a hurry*** and Room Service would ***take too long.***	G: 我急著要，而客房服務部要花太多時間。
H: There is a ***soft-drink*** machine in the elevator hall, ma'am.	H: 女士，電梯間有清涼飲料的販賣機。
G: Fine. I'll use that.	G: 好的，我就用那個。

活 用 練 習

☐1 You may *get change at the Cashier's desk*.

您可以在收納處換到零錢。

☐2 I'm afraid all the drinks are *sold out*, sir.

先生，恐怕所有的飲料都賣光了。

☐3 We don't provide *iced water* in Housekeeping.

客房管理部不供應冰水。

☐4 There is *a self-service ice-dispenser* near the elevator.

電梯附近有自助式的冰塊販賣機。

＊＊ *in a hurry* "匆忙地"

provide 〔prə'vaɪd〕 *v.* 供應；準備

soft-drink （不含酒精的）清涼飲料

elevator 〔'ɛləvetə 〕 *n.* 電梯

dispenser 〔dɪ'spɛnsə 〕 *n.* 販賣機

12

需要常備藥品時
Asking for Simple Medicine

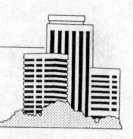

╭─── 〖 對話精華 〗 ───╮

◬ *I have a terrible headache*. Can you bring something for it?

　　我頭疼得厲害，可不可以拿點頭痛藥來？

◬ Please *take two tablets* three times a day after meals.

　　請每天三餐後服用兩片。

Dialogue：　*G* = **Guest** 旅客　　*H* = **Housekeeper** 管理員

G：　*I have a terrible headache.* Can you bring me something for it?

G：我頭疼得厲害，可不可以拿點頭痛藥來？

H：　Certainly, ma'am. We'll bring some medicine immediately.

H：好的，女士，我立刻送藥過去。

　　　(Goes to room)

　　　（到客房）

H：　Housekeeping. May I come in?

G：客房管理部，我可以進來嗎?

G：　Yes, of course.

H：當然可以。

H : I've brought your medicine, ma'am. ***Please take two tablets three times a day after meals.***

H：女士，我送來您的藥，請每天三餐後服用兩片。

G : Two tablets, three times a day after meals?

G：每天三餐後兩片嗎？

H : That's right, ma'am. I hope you have a good night.

H：對的，希望您好好睡一晚。

G : I'll try to, thanks.

G：我試試看，謝謝。

H : You're welcome, ma'am.

H：不客氣。

活用練習

1 I'm afraid *we do not stock medicine*, sir. Could you buy some at the Drug Store in the Lobby, please?

先生，我們恐怕並未儲備藥品，請到大廳的藥房去買些好嗎？

2 Shall I *call* a doctor *for* you? 要我幫您叫醫生嗎？

3 If there is anything else we can do for you, ***please do not hesitate to call*** "33".

若有其他我們可效勞的地方，請別猶豫，儘管撥"33"號。

4 Please let us know how you are. 請告訴我們您覺得如何？

** terrible〔'tɛrəbḷ〕*adj.* 非常的　　headache〔'hɛd,ek〕*n.* 頭痛
medicine〔'mɛdəsn̩〕*n.* 藥　　tablet〔'tæblɪt〕*n.* 錠劑
stock〔stɑk〕*v.* 備置　　hesitate〔'hɛzə,tet〕*v.* 猶豫

13 提供報紙・香煙等服務
Services to the Room Guest

‖ *對話精華* ‖

◉ Could you bring me an English newspaper, please?
請送一份英文報紙給我好嗎？

◉ We'll bring one *as soon as possible*.
我們會儘快送一份過去。

◉ It's free, sir. 免費的，先生。

Dialogue : *G* = **Guest** 旅客　*H* = **Housekeeper** 管理員

G : Could you bring me an
English newspaper, please?

G：請送一份英文報紙給我好嗎？

H : Certainly, sir. We'll bring
one *as soon as possible*.
Would you like an evening
newspaper tonight, too?

H：好的，先生，我們儘快送去。
您是否也要一份今晚的晚報
呢？

G : No, that's all right. How
much will it be?

G：不，那就夠了。要多少錢？

H : It's free, sir.

H：免費的，先生。

G : Fine. I'm sorry to *bother*
you but I'll need some
cigarettes, too.

G：好，抱歉麻煩你們，我還要
些香煙。

H : *That's no trouble at all,* sir. Which *brand* would you prefer?

H：一點也不麻煩，您喜歡哪一種牌子的？

G : Marlboro.

G：萬寶路。

H : How many packs will you need, sir?

H：您需要幾包？

G : Two, please, and just *add* them *to* the bill.

G：請送兩包，直接算進帳單裏好了。

H : I'm afraid cigarettes must *be paid for in cash*. Could you have the *exact* amount of NT$ 120 ready, please?

H：香煙恐怕得付現金，您身邊有台幣 120 元整嗎？

G : Sure.

G：有的

H : Thank you, sir. We will bring your newspaper and cigarettes *as soon as possible*.

H：先生，謝謝，我們會儘快把報紙和香煙送過去。

活用練習

1. There are **cigarette vending machines** in the Lobby and on the 10th Floor. 大廳及十樓有香煙自動販賣機。

2. I'm afraid **we do not shine shoes** in Housekeeping, sir. 客房管理部恐怕不提供擦鞋的服務。

3. There is some **shoeshine paper** in the closet, sir. 先生，衣櫥裏有擦鞋紙。

4. There is a **clothes** (**shoe**) **brush** in the closet (**wardrobe**). 衣櫥裏有衣（鞋）刷。

** **possible** 〔'pɑsəbḷ〕 *adj.* 可能的（ *as soon as possible* " 儘快 " ）
cigarette 〔,sɪgə'rɛt〕 *n.* 香煙
brand 〔brænd〕 *n.* 牌子；商標
pack 〔pæk〕 *n.* 包；一組
vending 〔'vɛndɪŋ〕 *n.* 販賣（ *vending machine* 自動販賣機）
brush 〔brʌʃ〕 *n.* 刷子
wardrobe 〔'wɔrd,rob〕 *n.* 衣櫥

14

電視故障時
When TV Is out of Order

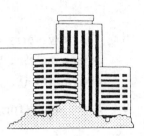

~ 〖對話精華〗 ~

◉ Did you *call for* service？您需要服務嗎？

◉ Yes, the television isn't *working*. 是的，電視壞了。

◉ I'll *take care of* it personally. 我會親自處理這件事。

Dialogue： *H* = **Housekeeper** 管理員　*G* = **Guest** 旅客

H： Housekeeping. May I come in?

H：客房管理部，我可以進來嗎?

G： Sure. Come on in.

G：當然。請進。

H： ***Did you call for service***, ma'am?

H：女士，您需要服務嗎？

G： Yes, the television isn't ***working***.

G：是的，電視壞了。

H： I'm very sorry, ma'am. An engineer will come and check it immediately.

H：非常抱歉，工程師會立刻前來檢查。

G： Oh, and ***another thing***, the people next door are very noisy.

G：對了，還有一件事，隔壁的人非常吵鬧。

H: I'm very sorry about the noise, ma'am. We will *check into* it.

H:女士，對此吵鬧我們非常抱歉，我們會調查這件事。

G: Fine, don't forget!

G:好的，別忘了。

H: *I'll take care of it personally*. Have a good night.

H:我會親自處理這件事，晚安。

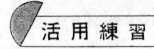 活 用 練 習

① We will bring a replacement immediately.
我們會立刻更換。

② I've brought the *spare fuse*. 我們拿備用保險絲來了。

③ I'm afraid the *capacity* is only 15 *amps* per two rooms. Could you use any high *wattage appliances separately*, please? 每兩個房間恐怕只有十五安培的電容量，請分開使用高電壓的器具好嗎？

** *call for* " 需要；需求 "
engineer 〔 ˏɛndʒə'nɪr 〕 n. 工程師；機械師　　*check into* " 調查 "
take care of " 處理；照顧 "　　**personally** 〔 'pɝsn̩lɪ 〕 adv. 親自地
spare 〔 spɛr 〕 adj. 備用的　　**fuse** 〔 fjuz 〕 n. 保險絲
capacity 〔 kə'pæsətɪ 〕 n. 電容器；容量
amp 〔 æmp 〕 n. 安培（計算電流強度之標準單位）
wattage 〔 'wɑtɪdʒ 〕 n. 瓦特數

15 被鎖在防火道之外時

Being Locked out of the Fire Exit

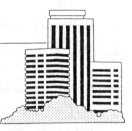

〖 對話精華 〗

◉ I'm outside *on the fire escape* and can't get in.
我被關在太平梯外面，進不去。

◉ Could you *step to the left* as the door opens out-wards. 因為門往外開，所以請站到左邊去好嗎？

Dialogue：*H* = **Housekeeper** 管理員　　*G* = **Guest** 旅客

H : Housekeeping. May I help you?

H：客房管理部，需要我效勞嗎？

G : I'm outside *on the fire escape* and can't get in. What shall I do?

G：我被關在太平梯外面，進不去。怎麼辦。

H : Which floor are you *on*, ma'am?

H：您在哪一樓，女士？

G : The 15th Floor.

G：十五樓。

H : Could you stay where you are, ma'am? We will send someone immediately.

H：請待在那裏好嗎？我們立刻派人過去。

　　(*Goes to 15th Floor*)

　　（到十五樓）

H : Hello? Is anyone there?　　H：喂？有人在那兒嗎？

G : Yes, I'm here.　　G：是的，我在這兒。

H : Could you *step to the left* as the door opens outwards, ma'am?　　H：因為門往外開，所以請站到左邊去好嗎？

G : Sure.　　G：好的。

　　　(*Opens door*)　　（打開門）

G : *Thank goodness you came*! I was beginning to *give up* hope.　　G：幸好你來了！我快開始放棄希望了。

H : I'm very sorry, ma'am, but for security reasons the fire doors cannot be opened from the outside.　　H：非常抱歉，但是基於安全理由，防火門是無法從外頭開啟的。

G : Oh, *is that the reason*?　　G：哦，是這樣嗎？

** *fire escape* 太平梯（為火警時便於逃出建築物之各種設備）
　　outwards〔'aʊtwədz〕*adv.* 向外的
　　give up "放棄"
　　security〔sɪ'kjʊrətɪ〕*n.* 安全

（ Paging Services ）

櫃枱爲旅客所提供的廣播服務，傳呼方式爲：

> *Paging for Mr. / Mrs. / Miss ～of Room ～ , you have a visitor（ telephone ）. Please contact with Front Desk（ operator ）. Thank you.*
>
> ～號房，～先生（小姐），您有訪客（電話）請與櫃枱（總機）連絡，謝謝！

此外，遭遇緊急事故（火警或空襲警報）時的廣播辭爲：

> *May I have your attention, please? This is an e-mergency. The place is on fire（ or air-raid ）now.* Please leave your room immediately and follow the emergency exit door. Withdraw this building im-mediately. Thank you for your cooperation.
>
> 緊急事故，請各位旅客注意，旅館發生火警（或空襲警報），請立刻離開房間，從太平門撤離這棟建築。謝謝您的合作。

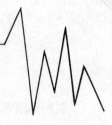

Fire

1. There is a small fire in the hotel.

2. Please do not worry, there is no danger.

3. The fire is **under control**.

4. Please keep calm.

5. Please follow me.

6. The **emergency exit** is this way.

7. Please do not use the elevators.

8. The elevators are not running.

9. Please do not worry, the fire is **out**.

10. Please **leave** your baggage **behind**.

11. Please leave the hotel.

12. Cover your nose and mouth with a wet towel so as not to **inhale** smoke or **fumes**.

13. Crouch or crawl along the wall, and **proceed** towards an emergency staircase free of flames.

火　災

1. 旅館裏發生一場小火災。

2. 請別擔心，沒有危險。

3. 火勢已壓下來了。

4. 請保持冷靜。

5. 請跟我來。

6. 緊急出口在這邊。

7. 請不要搭乘電梯。

8. 電梯停開了。

9. 請別擔心，火已經撲滅了。

10. 請將您的行李擱著。

11. 請離開旅館。

12. 請用溼毛巾掩住口鼻，以防吸入煙或毒氣。

13. 沿著牆壁蹲下或爬行，並向前推進到防火的緊急樓梯。

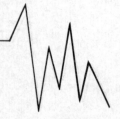

Earthquake

1. Please follow the **emergency instructions** broadcast throughout the hotel.

2. There has been a small **earthquake**.

3. **Keep away from** the window.

4. **Beware of** falling objects.

5. **Protect** your head.

6. It is dangerous to go outside.

7. It is dangerous to leave the hotel.

8. Please **get under** a table.

9. The building is quite safe in an earthquake of that size.

10. It is quite safe inside your room. Could you wait there **until it is over**?

11. This building has a flexible **earthquake-proof** structure.

** **broadcast** 〔'brɔd,kæst〕*v.* 廣播　　**earthquake** 〔'ɝθ,kwek〕*n.* 地震
beware 〔bɪ'wɛr〕*v.* 小心；留意　　**flexible** 〔'flɛksəbl̩〕*adj.* 柔靱的

地 震

1. 請遵守旅館播放的緊急指示。

2. 有一點小地震。

3. 遠離窗戶。

4. 小心墜落物。

5. 保護您的頭部。

6. （外頭很危險）請不要外出。

7. （離開旅館很危險）請不要離開旅館。

8. 請躲在桌子底下。

9. 在這種程度的地震下，這棟建築物很安全。

10. 待在房內很安全。請在那兒等候，直到（地震）停止好嗎？

11. 這棟建築有柔靭的防震構造。

** *earthquake-proof* 防震的
structure〔'strʌktʃɚ〕*n.* 構造

台灣地區觀光旅館住用率統計

資料來源：交通部觀光局

旅 館 類 別 Class	地　　　區 Area	住　用　率 Occupancy Rate
國際觀光旅館 International Tourist Hotels	台北市　Taipei	75.32 %
	台中市　Taichung	64.80 %
	高雄市　Kaohsiung	70.75 %
	花蓮市　Haulien	53.10 %
	桃竹苗 Taoyuan, Hsinchu & miaoli	63.36 %
	其他縣市　Others	56.04 %
	風景區　Scenic Area	59.92 %
	平均　Average	68.55 %
一般觀光旅館 Tourist Hotels	台北市　Taipei	76.94 %
	台中市　Taichung	74.15 %
	高雄市　Kaohsiung	00.00 %
	花蓮市　Haulien	44.81 %
	桃竹苗 Taoyuan, Hsinchu & miaoli	65.59 %
	其他縣市　Others	45.09 %
	風景區　Scenic Area	37.74 %
	平均　Average	60.08 %

Part 9

轉接電話
Telephone Operators

1

外線電話的處理
Outside Calls

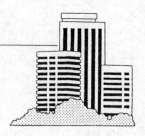

∬ 對話精華 ∬

◢ Could you *put* me *through* to Room #2614, please?
請幫我接通2614號房好嗎?

◢ I'd like to *speak with* Mr. Bramley.
我想請布蘭雷先生聽電話。

Dialogue ❶ : *C* = **Caller** 打電話的人　*O* = **Operator** 總機

C : Is this the President
Hotel?

C : 是統一大飯店嗎?

O : Speaking. (*Yes, it is.*)
May I help you?

O : 是的, 能為您效勞嗎?

C : Yes. ***Could you put me
through to Room*** #2614,
please?

C : 請幫我接通2614號房好嗎?

O : Certainly, sir. Just a
moment, please.

O : 好的, 先生, 請稍候。

Dialogue ❷ :

C : I'd like to ***speak with***
Mr. Bramley.

C : 我想請布蘭雷先生聽電話。

O： Is he a hotel guest, sir?　　　O：先生，他是旅館的客人嗎？

C： Yes.　　　C：是的。

O： How do you spell his
　　 name, please?　　　O：請問他的姓怎麼拼？

C： B.R.A.M.L.E.Y.　　　C：B、R、A、M、L、E、Y。

O： Just a moment, please.
　　 I'll check for you.……
　　 Thank you for waiting,
　　 sir. Mr. Bramley is
　　 staying in Room #1562.
　　 I'll connect you.

O：請稍等，我幫您查查看。……
……
讓您久等了，先生。布蘭雷
先生住1562號房，我幫您
接通。

① I'll *connect* you *with* the Front Reservation Desk.
　我幫您接通預約櫃枱。

② I'll connect you with the Restaurant Reservation Desk.
　我爲您接通餐廳的預約櫃枱。

③ Could you *repeat* that, please? 請再說一次好嗎？

④ Could you speak *more slowly*, please? 請說慢一點好嗎？

⑤ Could you speak *a little louder*, please? 請說大聲一點好嗎？

⑥ Who would you like to speak to? 您要請誰聽電話？

⑦ I'm afraid *the line is busy* (*engaged*). 恐怕在佔線中。

⑧ I'm afraid **the line is bad**. 恐怕線路不通。

⑨ I'm afraid you have the wrong number. 您恐怕撥錯號碼了。

⑩ We have no room with that number. All our rooms have three or four digit numbers. Who are you calling, please? 我們並沒有那個號碼的房間，我們所有的房間都是三位數或四位數字，請問您要找誰？

⑪ I'm afraid there's no guest (employee/shop/restaurant……) **with that name**. 恐怕沒有叫那個名字的客人（職員／商店／餐廳……）。

**　**operator** 〔ˈɑpəˌretɚ〕 *n*. 總機；（電話之）接線生
　　connect 〔kəˈnɛkt〕 *v*. 接通
　　restaurant 〔ˈrɛstərənt〕 *n*. 餐廳
　　repeat 〔rɪˈpit〕 *v*. 重說；重做
　　employee 〔ɪmˈplɔɪ‧i〕 *n*. 職員

客房沒有人回應時
No Reply from the Room

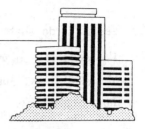

∥ 對話精華 ∥

◉ I'm afraid *there's no reply from* Room #3510.
　3510 號房恐怕沒人接電話。

◉ Could you *try* again? 請再試一次好嗎？

Dialogue： *C* = **Caller** 打電話的人　*O* = **Operator** 總機

C : Hello. Can I speak to Mr.
　　Franks in Room #3510,
　　please?

C : 喂，請幫我找 3510 號房的
　　法蘭克斯先生聽電話好嗎？

O : Certainly, sir. Just a
　　moment, please. ……
　　Thank you for waiting.
　　I'm afraid **there's no
　　reply from** Room #3510.

O : 好的，先生，請稍候。……

　　讓您久等了，3510 號房恐怕
　　沒人接電話。

C : Could you try again?

C : 請再試一次好嗎？

O : Certainly, sir. Just a
　　moment, please. ……
　　Thank you for waiting.
　　I'm afraid there is still
　　no reply. Would you like
　　to **leave a message**?

O : 好的，先生，請稍等。……

　　讓您久等了，恐怕還是沒人
　　接電話，您要留話嗎？

C : Yes, I'll do that.

O : I'll **connect** you **with** the Message Desk. Just a moment, please.

C：好的。我要留話。

O：我幫您接通傳話櫃枱，請稍等。

△旅館會議廳：供商品展示、業務會報及工商聚餐。

廣播呼叫客人
Paging a Guest

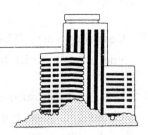

〄 對話精華 〄

◬ Would you like to *leave a message*. 您要留話嗎？

◬ Could you *page* him for me? 請幫我廣播叫他好嗎？

Dialogue : *C* = **C**aller 打電話的人　　*O* = **O**perator 總機

C : Is this the Holiday Hotel?

O : Speaking. May I help you?

C : Yes. Could you *put* me *through* to Mr. Mercer in Room #1513, please?

O : Certainly, sir. ……
Thank you for waiting, sir. I'm afraid there is no reply from Room #1513. Would you like to *leave a message*?

C : Well, I'm sure he's in the hotel. Could you *page* him for me?

C：是假期大飯店嗎？

O：是的，能為您效勞嗎？

C：請幫我接通 1513 號房的馬撒先生好嗎？

O：好的，先生。……
讓您久等了，1513 室恐怕沒人接電話，您要留話嗎？

O：哦，我確定他在旅館裏，請幫我廣播叫他好嗎？

O : Certainly, sir. Where do you think he will be?

O：好的，先生。您認為他會在哪裏呢？

C : He's probably having lunch. Could you page the restaurants, please?

C：他可能在吃中飯，請向餐廳呼叫好嗎？

O : Do you know *which restaurant he is likely to be in*?

O：您知道他可能在哪個餐廳嗎？

C : I've no idea.

C：不清楚。

O : I'm afraid we can only page the *public places*.

O：我們恐怕只能向公共場所呼叫了。

C : Fine. Do that then, please!

C：好的，那麼就麻煩你了！

O : May I have his full name?

O：請告訴我他的全名，好嗎？

C : Tom Mercer.

C：湯姆・馬撒。

O : Mr. Tom Mercer. Thank you, sir. Could you hold the line, please?

O：湯姆・馬撒先生。謝謝您，先生。請別掛斷好嗎？

Paging Mr. Tom Mercer, Paging Mr. Tom Mercer. Please *pick up* the nearest House phone for Operator No. 5. Thank you.

來賓湯姆・馬撒先生，來賓湯姆・馬撒先生，請利用最近的內線電話和第五線的總機聯絡，謝謝。

** *leave a message* "留話；傳言"   *likely* 〔ˈlaɪklɪ〕 *adj.* 有可能的
page 〔pedʒ〕 *v.* (在旅館、俱樂部中)喊出其名字以尋找(某人)

4

被呼叫客人沒有回應時
No Reply
from the Paged Guest

〖 對話精華 〗

◎ We have paged Mr. Mercer but *he didn't pick up the phone*. 我們已呼叫過馬撒先生了，但是他沒有打電話來。

◎ Could you *try* there, please? 請試試那兒好嗎？

Dialogue : *O* = **Operator** 總機 *C* = **Caller** 打電話的人

O : I'm very sorry to have kept you waiting. We have paged Mr. Mercer but *he did not pick up the phone*. Shall we try again ?

O : 對不起，讓您久等了。我們已呼叫過馬撒先生，但是他沒有打電話來，要我們再試一次嗎？

C : Yes. I've just remembered. He might be in the Garden Lounge. Could you try there, please?

C : 好的，我剛想起來，他可能在花園休息室裏，請試試那兒好嗎？

O : Certainly, sir. I'll *connect* you *with* the Garden Lounge.

O : 好的，先生。我替您接通花園休息室。

** **lounge** 〔lauŋdʒ〕 *n.* 休息室

抵達時外線電話已掛斷
Outside Caller Being Cut off

〚對話精華〛

◉ I'm afraid *your party was cut off*.
　對方恐怕已經掛斷了。

◉ Did he give his name? 他有沒有留下名字？

◉ I'm very sorry *we couldn't help you*.
　非常抱歉我們無能為力。

Dialogue : *O* = **O**perator 總機　*G* = **G**uest 旅客

　　　　(*Operator speaks to*　　　　（總機對呼叫的客人說話）
　　　　Paged Guest)

O : Mr. Mercer? There was a　　　O : 馬撒先生嗎？有一通您的電
　　call for you but I'm afraid　　　　話，但是對方恐怕已經掛斷
　　your party was cut off.　　　　　了。

G : *That's a nuisance*! Did he　　G : 糟糕！他有沒有留下名字？
　　give his name?

O : I'm afraid not, sir. I'm　　　O : 恐怕沒有，先生。非常抱歉
　　very sorry we couldn't　　　　　我們無能為力。
　　help you.

G : It couldn't be helped.
Thanks anyway.

G ：那也沒有用，無論如何還是
謝謝你。

O : You're welcome, sir.

O ：不客氣，先生。

** ***cut off*** *= hang up* "掛斷電話"
nuisance〔'njusn̩s〕*n.* 討厭之人或物

6
客房間的通話與外線電話
Room-to-room & Outside Calls

╭─ 〖對話精華〗 ─╮

◐ I'd like to *call my friend in his room*.
　我想打電話到朋友的房間。

◐ *Please dial* 60 and then the room number.
　請先撥 60 再撥房間號碼。

Dialogue : *O* = Operator 總機　　*G* = Guest 旅客

O : This is the Operator.
　　May I help you?

O : 總機，能為您效勞嗎？

G : Yes. I'd like to call my
　　friend in his room. What
　　shall I do?

G : 我想打電話到朋友的房間，
　　該怎麼打？

O : Do you know the room
　　number, sir?

O : 先生，您知道他的房間號碼
　　嗎？

G : Yes, it's #814.

G : 知道，814 號房。

O : For 3 *digit* rooms in the
　　Main Building, please dial
　　60 and then the room
　　number.

O : 要打到主要大樓三位數的房
　　間，請先撥 60 再撥房間號
　　碼。

G : I see, well, *what about* outside calls? 　　　　G：我明白了，那麼，外線電話呢？

O : For calls inside Taipei, please dial 0 first and then the number. 　　　　O：打台北市內電話，請先撥 0 再撥電話號碼。

G : What about outside Taipei? I'd like to call Tainan. 　　　　G：打到台北市以外呢？我想打到台南。

O : For calls outside Taipei, please dial 0 and then the *area code* and number. 　　　　O：要打到台北市以外，請先撥 0 再撥區域號碼和電話號碼。

G : Fine. Thanks a lot. 　　　　G：好的，非常謝謝。

O : You're welcome, sir. 　　　　O：不客氣，先生。

1　For calls inside Taipei, the *area code* of 02 is not necessary. 打到台北市內，不必打區域號碼02。

2　*There is no charge for house calls.* 內線電話不收費。

3　All house calls are free. 所有的內線電話均免費。

** **digit** 〔ˈdɪdʒɪt〕*n*. 數字　　　*area code* "區域號碼"

7

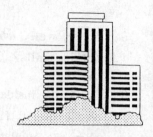

早晨叫醒電話
The Morning Call

〃對話精華〃

⚉ I'd like to *be woken up* tomorrow morning.
明天早上想請你叫我起床。

⚉ *At what time*? 幾點呢？

Dialogue : *O* = Operator 總機　*G* = Guest 旅客

O : This is the Operator. May I help you?

O：總機，能為您效勞嗎？

G : Yes, I'd like to *be woken up* tomorrow morning.

G：明天早上想請你叫我起床。

O : Certainly, sir. At what time?

O：好的，先生。幾點？

G : At around 7:30 a.m.

G：七點半左右。

O : We have *a computer wake-up service*. Please dial 5 first and then the time. For 7:30 a.m. dial 5 and then 0730 for the time. *There must be five digits in the final number*.

O：我們有電腦叫醒服務，請先撥五再撥時間。早晨七點半，撥五再撥時間0730。所撥的號碼總共必須是五位數字。

G : 50730. I see.

G : 50730，我懂了。

O : That's right, sir. Our computer will *record* the time and your room number.

O : 對的，先生。我們的電腦會記錄時間和您的房間號碼。

G : Thank you.

G : 謝謝。

O : You're welcome, sir. *Have a good night.*

O : 不客氣，晚安。

① At what time shall we call you? 我們該什麼時候叫您起床？

② Please dial your new wake-up time. *The computer will cancel the old time.*
　　請撥您改換的起床時間，電腦會刪除原來的時間。

③ We use a twenty-four hour clock. 我們採用二十四小時制。

** **woken** 〔'wokən〕 *v.* （ wake 的過去分詞 ）叫醒
　 record 〔rɪ'kɔrd〕 *v.* 記錄
　 cancel 〔'kænsl〕 *v.* 刪除；取消

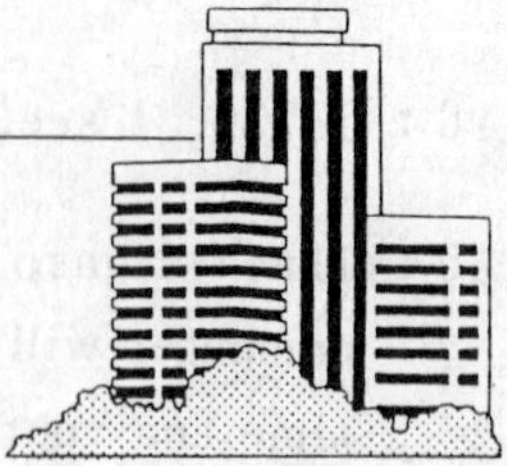

8 代理通話服務
Answering Service

〖對話精華〗

▲ Could you *place the call* for me?
能不能幫我打這通電話呢？

▲ *What number* are you calling, please?
請問您要打幾號？

Dialogue: *G* = **Guest** 旅客 *O* = **Operator** 總機

G: Operator. I've tried calling a number in Taipei but I can't understand what they're saying. ***Could you place the call for me?***	G: 總機，我試過在台北打電話，但是我不懂他們說什麼，能不能幫我打這通電話呢？
O: Certainly, sir. I'd ***be glad to*** help you. What number are you calling, please?	O: 好的，先生，很樂意爲您效勞。請問您要打幾號？
G: 433-8251.	G: 433-8251。
O: Is this a company number or a private number?	O: 這是公司電話號碼還是私人電話號碼？
G: A company one.	G: 是一家公司的電話號碼。

O : May I have the name of
the company, please?

O：請告訴我該公司的 名號好嗎？

G : Yes, it's the Her-han
Engineering Company.

G：好的，叫做和漢工程公司 。

O : Who would you like to
speak to, please?

O：請 問您想和誰通話 ？

G : Mr. Wang of the Sales
Department.

G：銷售部的王先生 。

O : Do you know his *extension
number* or his *first name*?

O：您知道他的內線號碼或名字
嗎 ？

G : Not the extension number
but I think his name is
Ming-uei.

G：我不知道內線號碼，但是我
想他的名字叫明威 。

O : May I have your name and
room number, please?

O：請告訴我您的 名字 和房間號
碼好嗎？

G : Yes, my name's Robbins
and I'm in Room #724.

G：好的，我叫羅賓斯，住 724
號房 。

O : Thank you. Could you *hang
up*, please, and *I'll call
you back*?

O：謝謝，請先掛斷，我再給您
回電好嗎？

**　company〔ˈkʌmpənɪ〕*n.* 公司　　**private**〔ˈpraɪvɪt〕*adj.* 私人的
　　engineering〔͵ɛndʒəˈnɪrɪŋ〕*n.* 工程學
　　extension〔ɪkˈstɛnʃən〕*n.*（電話）分機
　　hang up "掛斷電話"

⑨ 對電話佔線的抱怨
Complaint about a Busy Line

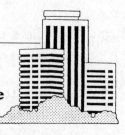

∥ 對話精華 ∥

◎ Shall I ask him to call you *when the line is free.*
線路暢通後，我請他打電話給您好嗎？

◎ Each time *the line was engaged.* 每次都佔線。

Dialogue ❶ : *G =* Guest 旅客　*O =* Operator 總機

(During Peak Hours)　　　　（尖峯時間）

G : Operator. I've been trying to ***get through to*** the Assistant Manager's Desk for the last ten minutes. The line has been continuously ***engaged.*** Why is it taking so long?

G : 總機，十分鐘來我一直試圖接通副理辦公室，該線持續佔用，爲什麼要花這麼久時間呢？

O : I'm very sorry to hear that, sir. I'm afraid ***it is often the case during peak hours.*** Shall I ask him to call you when the line is *free*?

O : 很抱歉聽您這麼說。尖峯時間恐怕常有這種情況，線路暢通後，我請他打電話給您，好嗎？

G : Yes, do that.   G：好的，麻煩你。

Dialogue ❷ :

    (*Simultaneous Incoming*   （同時打進來的電話）
    Calls)

G : ***Put me through to Room***   G：請幫我接通4312號房。
    #4312, please.

O : Certainly, ma'am. ……   O：好的，女士。……
    Thank you for waiting,   勞您久等了，4312號房可
    ma'am. I'm afraid there's   能沒有人接聽。
    no reply from Room #4312.

G : That's not possible! I've   G：不可能！我前十分鐘內已打
    called twice in the last ten   過兩次，而且每次都佔線。
    minutes and ***each time the***
    line was engaged.

O : I'm sorry, ma'am, but if   O：對不起，女士，如果同時有
    there are two incoming calls   兩通電話打進來，我們常會
    at the same time, we often   聽到佔線的信號聲。
    hear a busy signal.

G : Oh, ***is that the reason***? I   G：哦，是那樣嗎？我明白了。
    understand.

** **peak** 〔pik〕*adj.* 顛峯的；最高的
    continuously 〔kən'tɪnjʊəslɪ〕*adv.* 不斷地；連續地
    engage 〔ɪn'gedʒ〕*v.* 講話中；佔線
    simultaneous 〔͵saɪml̩'tenɪəs〕*adj.* 同時的   **signal** 〔'sɪgn̩l〕*n.* 信號

10 越洋收聽人付費電話
Incoming Collect Call from Overseas

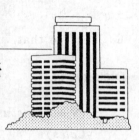

╭─〈〈 對話精華 〉〉─────────────────╮
│   │
│ ◉ Is this *a paid call*? 這是已付費電話嗎? │
│   │
│ ◉ It's *collect*. 這是接聽人付費的電話。   │
│   │
╰──────────────────────────╯

Dialogue : *IO* = **International Operator** 國際台接線生

　　　　　　O = **Operator**（旅館）總機

IO : This is Bombay calling. *I have a call for* Mr. Tom Smith.

IO : 這裏是孟買,有一通湯姆‧史密斯先生的電話。

O : Bombay for Mr. Tom Smith. Do you know his room number, please?

O : 從孟買打給湯姆‧史密斯先生的電話,請問您知道他的房間號碼嗎?

IO : Yes, it's #3820.

IO : 知道,3820 號房。

O : Thank you. Is this a *paid call*?

O : 謝謝。這是已付費電話嗎?

IO : It's *collect*.

IO : 是由接聽人付費的電話。

O : May I know *who is calling*, please?

O : 請問是誰打的電話?

IO : Yes. Pradip Patel.

IO : 普雷迪普‧斐達。

O : How do you spell that, please?

O：請問怎麼拼？

10 : Pakistan P, America A, Tokyo T, England E, London L.

10：巴基斯坦的 P ，美國的 A ， 東京的 T ，英國的 E ，倫敦 的 L 。

O : Mr. Pradip Patel. Thank you. Just a moment, please.

O：普雷迪普・斐達先生，謝謝， 請稍等。

(calls Room #3820)

（打到3820 號房）

May I *speak to* Mr. Tom Smith, please?

請湯姆・史密斯先生聽電話 好嗎？

G : *Speaking.* What can I do for you?

G：我就是，有什麼事嗎？

O : This is the Hotel Operator. *I have a collect call from Mr. Pradip Patel in Bombay.* Will you *accept the charges*?

O：這裏是旅館總機，有一通普 雷迪普・斐達先生從孟買打 來的接聽人付費電話，您願 意付款嗎？

G : Yes; of course.

G：當然願意。

O : Thank you. Could you hold the line, please?

O：謝謝，請別掛斷好嗎？

(Speaks to the International Operator)

（對國際台接線生講話）

Hello. Mr. Smith will accept the call. Could you give me your **operator number**, please?

喂,史密斯先生要接這通電話,請告訴我您的總機號碼好嗎?

10: Yes, it's 23.

10:好的,23號。

0: Thank you. My number is 54. Could you give me the time and the charges after the call, please?

0:謝謝,我的號碼是54號,通完話之後,請告訴我通話時間及費用好嗎?

10: Yes, of course.

10:當然好。

0: Thank you. **Go ahead**, please.

0:謝謝,請說。

1 "Your call to Los Angeles **lasted** …… minutes. It will cost …… N.T. dollars. We will **add** it **to** your final room bill."
您打到洛杉磯的電話持續了～分鐘,費用～台幣,我們將一併加算在最終的宿費帳單上。

2 Who is **paying for** the call? 由誰付這通電話的費用?

3 Will you accept the call? 您要接這通電話嗎?

** **Bombay** 〔bɑm'be〕 *n*. 孟買
   collect 〔kə'lɛkt〕 *adj*. 由接聽人 (收件人) 付款的
   Pakistan 〔͵pækɪ'stæn〕 *n*. 巴基斯坦
   Los Angeles 〔lɔs'ændʒələs〕 *n*. 洛杉磯

11
越洋叫人電話
Outgoing Overseas Person-to-person Call

〖對話精華〗

◉ I'd like to *make an international call*.
我想打一通國際電話。

◉ A *person-to-person* or a *station call*, sir?
先生，您打叫人或是叫號電話呢？

Dialogue： *G* = **Guest** 旅客　*O* = **Operator** 總機

G： Hello. Operator?

O： Speaking. May I help you?

G： Yes. I'd like to *make an international call*.

O： Certainly, sir. Which country are you calling?

G： Switzerland.

O： Is this a *paid call*?

G： Yes.

O： A *person-to-person* or a *station call*, sir?

G：喂，總機嗎？

O：是的，能為您效勞嗎？

G：是的，我想打一通國際電話。

O：好的，先生。您要打到哪一國？

G：瑞士。

O：這是由您付費的電話嗎？

G：是的。

O：先生，您打叫人或是叫號電話呢？

G : Person-to-person.

G：叫人電話。

O : Could you tell me the party's full name and telephone number, please?

O：請告訴我對方的全名和電話號碼好嗎？

G : Yes, it's Grace Pereira and the number is Lausanne 49680.

G：好的，是葛麗絲‧斐里拉，電話號碼是洛桑49680號。

O : Mrs. Grace Pereira at Lausanne 49680.

O：洛桑49680的葛麗絲‧斐里拉太太。

G : That's right.

G：對的。

O : May I have your name and room number, please?

O：請問您貴姓和房間號碼？

G : Yes, it's Zachary and I'm in Room #834.

G：我是撒查理，住834號房。

O : Mr. Zachary in Room #834.

O：834號房的撒查理先生。

G : That's right.

G：對的。

O : Could you *hang up*, please and we will *call* you *back*?

O：請掛斷，我們給您回電好嗎？

Ⓖ   Ⓖ   Ⓖ

O : May I speak to Mr. Zachary, please?

可以請撒查理先生聽電話嗎？

G : Zachary, speaking.

G：我就是撒查理。

O : This is the Hotel Operator. The Overseas Operator is *on the line*. Go ahead, please.

O：我是旅館總機，已接通國際電信台，請說。

** **Switzerland** 〔ˈswɪtsələnd〕 *n.* 瑞士

person-to-person call 叫人電話

station call 叫號電話

Lausanne 〔loˈzɑn〕 *n.* 洛桑

12

直撥叫號電話
Station Call-Direct Dialling

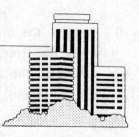

─── ∬ **對話精華** ∬ ───

◉ *You may call direct from your room*, sir.
　先生，您可以直接由客房打出去。

◉ The country codes are listed in the Services
Directory in your room.
　國家代號列在您房間裏的服務指南上。

Dialogue : *O* = **Operator** 總機　*G* = **Guest** 旅客

O : This is the Hotel Operator. May I help you?

O：旅館總機，能為您效勞嗎？

G : Yes. I'd like to *make an*
overseas call.

G：我要打一通越洋電話。

O : You may call *direct* from
your room, sir. It is
cheaper than *booking* it
through the operator.

O：先生，您可以直接由客房打
出去。這樣比經由總機打出
要來得便宜。

G : Oh. I didn't know that.

G：哦，我不曉得。

O : The country codes are
listed in the Services
Directory in your room.
Please dial 4001 before
the country code and then
dial the *area code* and
number. Please do not
dial 0 before the entire
number *as you would for
an outside call.*

O : 國家代號列在您房間裏的服
務指南上。請於國家代號前
先撥4001，然後再撥區域
號碼及電話號碼。在撥整個
號碼前面，不用像打外線電
話一樣地先撥0。

G : I see. 4001 and then
country code, area code
and number.

G : 我懂了，先撥4001再撥國
家代號、區域號碼和電話號
碼。

O : That is right, sir.

O : 是的，先生。

G : Thank you very much.

G : 非常謝謝。

O : You're welcome, sir.

O : 不客氣，先生。

1 You are charged by the *6 second unit* and not the *3 minute
unit* as for person-*to*-person calls.
　您打叫人電話是以每6秒鐘爲單位計費而不是以每3分鐘爲單位計
　費。

2 The country codes are listed in the Services Directory in
your room. *You can make a call directly.*
　國家代號列在您房間的服務指南上，您可以直接打出去。

③ I'm afraid all calls to ……must *go through* the Operator.
所有打到～的電話恐怕都必須透過總機打出。

④ Would you like me to *place* the *call* for you?
要我幫您打這通電話嗎？

⑤ *Excuse me for asking* but which country are you calling?
對不起，請問您是要打到哪個國家？

** **overseas** 〔'ovə'siz〕 *adj.* 海外的；外國的
directory 〔də'rɛktərɪ〕 *n.* 指南；寶鑑

13 國際電話費用
International Rates

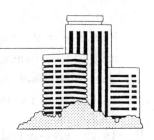

╭─╮ ∥ **對話精華** ∥ ╭─╮

◑ Could you tell me *the rates for calls to* the States?
能不能告訴我打電話到美國的費用呢？

◑ For the *mainland* U.S.A.? 打到美國本土嗎？

Dialogue: *G* = **Guest** 旅客　　*O* = **Operator** 總機

G : Operator. Could you tell me the *rates* for calls to the States?

G：總機，能不能告訴我打電話到美國的費用呢？

O : Certainly, sir. For the *mainland* U.S.A.?

O：好的，是打到美國本土嗎？

G : No. it's Honolulu.

G：不，檀香山。

O : Just a moment, please. I'll check it for you.... Thank you for waiting, sir. A three minute person-to-person call is NT$474 *on weekdays* and NT$357 on Sundays. A station call is

O：請稍等，我幫您查一下。……先生，讓您久等了。叫人電話平日三分鐘台幣474元，星期日357元。叫號電話平日396元，星期日297元，超過時間每分鐘加收119元。

NT$396 on weekdays and
NT$297 on Sundays. For
each *additional minute*, the
charge is NT$119.

G : Is there a special night
rate?

G：有夜間特別收費嗎？

O : *Not if you go through the
Operator*, sir.

O：經由總機則沒有特別收費，
先生。

① What is the price of a call to Anchorage?
打電話到安克拉治的費用是多少？

② Each extra minute costs NT$.....
每超過一分鐘加計新台幣～元。

③ London is 8 hours behind Taipei.
倫敦的時間比台北慢了8小時。

④ Canada is 11 and a half to 17 hours behind Taiwan depending
on the time zone.
加拿大時間依時區比台灣慢十一個半到十七個小時。

** **mainland**〔'menlənd〕*n.* 本土；大陸
Honolulu〔,hɑnə'lulu〕*n.* 檀香山
weekday〔'wik,de〕*n.* 平日；星期日以外的任何一天
Anchorage〔'æŋkərɪdʒ〕*n.* 安克拉治
depend on "視…而定"

14

抱怨線路有雜音
Complaints about Noise on the Line

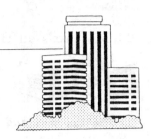

╢ **對話精華** ╟

◐ I'm not going to *pay for the call*!
我不付這通電話費！

◐ Shall I *connect* you *with* the International Operator?
要我為您和國際電信局聯絡嗎？

Dialogue： *G =* **Guest** 旅客　　*O =* **Operator** 總機

G : Operator. I've just *made a call to* Los Angeles but I couldn't hear anything. I'm not going to pay for the call!

G：總機，我剛打過電話到洛杉磯，可是我什麼也聽不到，我不付這通電話費！

O : I see, sir. How long was your call?

O：我知道了，先生。您的電話打了多久？

G : Two minutes *at the most*.

G：頂多兩分鐘。

O : Our computer shows that you spoke for four minutes and thirty seconds, sir. Shall I *connect* you *with* the International Operator?

O：先生，我們的電腦顯示您講了四分鐘三十秒，要我為您和國際電信局聯絡嗎？

G：No, that's all right.　　　　G：不用了，沒有關係。

① The line was **bad**. 線路故障。

② The line was **noisy**. 線路有雜音。

③ There was a lot of **interference** on the line.
該線路受到很多干擾。

④ There was a lot of **static** on the line. 該線路曾多次中斷。

⑤ There was a *crackling／humming／buzzing* noise.
有噼啪／嗡嗡／喳喳聲。

⑥ Their voice was **too faint to hear**. 聲音太微弱，聽不清楚。

⑦ I was **cut off** in the middle of the call.
我的電話中途被切斷。

⑧ I had a **crossed line**. 我的電話被岔線。

**　interference 〔͵ɪntɚˈfɪrəns〕*n*. （無線電）干擾
　　static 〔ˈstætɪk〕*adj*. 靜止的
　　crackle 〔ˈkrækl̩〕*n*. 噼啪聲
　　faint 〔fent〕*adj*. 微弱的

新旅館英語

修　　編／劉宜芳

發　行　所／學習出版有限公司　　　　☎ (02) 2704-5525

郵 撥 帳 號／0512727-2 學習出版社帳戶

登 記 證／局版台業 2179 號

印　刷　所／裕強彩色印刷有限公司

台 北 門 市／台北市許昌街 10 號 2 F　　☎ (02) 2331-4060・2331-9209

台灣總經銷／紅螞蟻圖書有限公司　　　☎ (02) 2795-3656

美國總經銷／Evergreen Book Store　　☎ (818) 2813622

本公司網址　www.learnbook.com.tw

電 子 郵 件　learnbook@learnbook.com.tw

售價：新台幣二百八十元正

2008 年 7 月 1 日二版一刷

ISBN 978-957-519-981-4